STORIES TO TELL TO CHILDREN

Stories

Eighth Edition

Revised and edited by

Laura E. Cathon

Marion McC. Haushalter

Virginia A. Russell

Margaret Hodges, *Consultant*

TO TELL TO
Children
A Selected List

Published for

Carnegie Library of Pittsburgh Children's Services

by the UNIVERSITY OF PITTSBURGH PRESS

Copyright © 1974, Carnegie Library of Pittsburgh
All rights reserved
Feffer and Simons, Inc., London
Manufactured in the United States of America

Library of Congress Cataloging in Publication Data

Pittsburgh. Carnegie Library.
  Stories to tell to children.

  1. Children's stories—Bibliography. 2. Holidays—
Bibliography. I. Cathon, Laura E., ed. II. Haushalter,
Marion McC., birth date, ed. III. Russell, Virginia A.,
birth date, ed. IV. Pittsburgh. Carnegie Library.
Children's Services. V. Title.
Z1037.P693 1974   028.5   73-13317
ISBN 0-8229-3280-6
ISBN 0-8229-5246-7 (pbk.)

Text and cover decorations by Ralph Creasman

Contents

Preface   *vii*

Introduction   *ix*

Stories of Special Interest to Preschool Children   *3*

Stories of Special Interest to Children from Six to Ten
    Years of Age   *17*

Stories of Special Interest to Older Boys and Girls   *51*

Stories for Holiday Programs   *67*

        Christmas   *67*

        Easter   *73*

        Halloween   *74*

        Jewish Holidays   *78*

        Mother's Day   *79*

        New Year's Day   *79*

        Patriotic Days   *80*

        St. Patrick's Day   *81*

        St. Valentine's Day   *81*

        Thanksgiving   *82*

Aids for the Storyteller   *85*

Classified List of Stories   *87*

        Action Stories   *87*

        Afro-Americans   *87*

        American Indians   *87*

        Animal Stories   *87*

Classified List of Stories (*continued*)
> Ballad Stories   *89*
> Bible Stories   *90*
> Blindness   *90*
> Cumulative and Repetitive Stories   *90*
> Dragons   *90*
> Ecology   *91*
> Epics and Sagas   *91*
> Ethical and Social Values   *91*
> Fables   *92*
> Flight   *92*
> Folktales by Country   *92*
> Ghosts   *100*
> Giants   *100*
> Gypsies   *100*
> Humorous Stories   *101*
> Jews   *102*
> Legends   *102*
> Modern Imaginative Stories   *103*
> Modern Realistic Stories   *106*
> Music Stories   *106*
> Myths   *107*
> Saints   *107*
> Stories by Country   *107*
> Tall Tales   *108*
> Toys   *108*
> Witches and Wizards   *109*

Alphabetical List of Stories   *111*

Books Referred to in the Foregoing Lists   *125*

Preface

STORYTELLING HOURS have been a regular feature in the Carnegie Library of Pittsburgh since 1899. The majority of stories listed on the following pages have been selected from those still being told in story hours and tested with children for interest, popularity, and quality.

The first edition, published in 1916, was compiled by Miss Edna Whiteman, Supervisor of Storytelling at that time; the second, third, and fourth editions, issued in 1918, 1921, and 1926, were revised by Miss Margaret Carnegie and Miss Elizabeth Nesbitt. The fifth edition, printed in 1932, was compiled and revised by Miss Esther Fleming, under the direction of Miss Elva S. Smith, then Head of the Boys and Girls Department.

The sixth edition, printed in 1950, was revised and edited by Miss Laura E. Cathon, Miss Kathryn Kohberger, and Miss Virginia A. Russell. The compilation of the seventh edition (1960) was accomplished by a committee of children's librarians at the Carnegie Library of Pittsburgh: Mrs. Margaret Hodges, Miss Virginia A. Russell, and Miss Laura E. Cathon, Chairman. Miss Elizabeth Nesbitt, Associate Dean, Carnegie Library School of Carnegie Institute of Technology, served as consultant. The sixth and seventh editions were compiled under the direction of Miss Virginia Chase, Head, Boys and Girls Department.

Continued demand for the Pittsburgh list, *Stories to Tell to Children*, has made an eighth edition necessary. This eighth edition has been compiled by a committee: Mrs. Marion McC. Haushalter, Head, Central Children's Division; Miss Virginia A. Russell, Children's Librarian, East Liberty Branch; and Miss Laura E. Cathon, Coordinator, Children's Services, Chairman. Mrs. Margaret Hodges, Associate Professor, Graduate School of Library and Information Sciences, University of Pittsburgh, served as consultant. Miss Helen Yee, Secretary, Children's Services, has given valuable service to the committee.

A number of new subject headings have been added to the eighth edition. Stories and folktales of the emerging nations, especially the countries of Africa and Southeast Asia, are being published in increasing numbers. A great many of these were not available for the earlier editions. Some titles found in earlier editions have been deleted and new ones added. The list of sources has been revised and greatly enlarged.

ANTHONY A. MARTIN
Director, Carnegie Library of Pittsburgh

Introduction

IN THE following lists the stories are grouped according to their interest to children of different ages. The stories listed in the section "Stories of Special Interest to Preschool Children" have been used successfully with many Head Start and pre-primary groups. The stories with the symbol *pb* (for picture book) have been especially useful for deaf children, for whom pictures help carry the message of the story, and for younger children.

Because no definite lines can be drawn, each group includes stories which may be enjoyed by children either older or younger than the headings indicate. Many stories in the sections "Stories of Special Interest to Children from Six to Ten Years of Age" and "Stories of Special Interest to Older Boys and Girls" are suitable for telling to young adult and adult audiences. The stories with ethnic backgrounds which are a part of traditional literature have been told to adult groups with success. Storytelling has great therapeutic value for the handicapped and the aged.

Special lists of stories by holidays are included. In the section "Stories for Holiday Programs" stories suitable for preschool and primary grades are indicated by the symbol *y*.

In order that a story suited to a given purpose may be found easily, the stories in each of the four sections are characterized as fables, folktales, legends, myths, etc. A "modern imaginative story" or "modern realistic story" in this list indicates a story by a modern author, not necessarily a story with a modern setting. Special attention is called to headings in the classified index which follows the lists. The folktales and stories by country have been identified by specific country rather than by continent, with the exception of certain stories from Africa which have been classified by continent because the country could not be ascertained.

Many stories are suitable for broadcasting by radio or television. With adaptation to emphasize action and a strong story line, these stories can be told within the framework of a limited time program. Arrangements must be made with the individual publisher to use copyrighted material on radio or television.

When a story is *also called* by titles markedly different from the main entry, it is so indicated.

PARALLELS AND VARIANTS

Parallel or similar stories are given only when these are also acceptable for storytelling. Variants of the main entry are stories having the same theme and nationality background; parallels are stories having the same theme but with a different nationality background.

SOURCES

Not all known sources are given. The arrangement of sources is alphabetical by author. As a rule, paging has not been given, but it has been added when a story is a part of a chapter and might not be found readily.

A few out-of-print books have been retained in the list when no satisfactory substitutes have been found. In most cases copies are still available in libraries.

Films and records for use in storytelling hours are not included, since these are listed in other sources, and since films and records become unavailable quickly. References to sources for films and records are given in the section "Aids for the Storyteller."

Book prices have not been added, because they are subject to change. Full bibliographic information for books can be obtained from *Books in Print*, R. R. Bowker Company.

STORYTELLING AIDS

A list of books and articles on the techniques and values of storytelling is included in this edition.

STORIES TO TELL TO CHILDREN

KEY TO SYMBOLS

pb Indicates a picture book edition.
 y Indicates a holiday story suitable for young children.

Stories of Special Interest to Preschool Children

The Adventurous Mouse (folktale)
Price. *The Rich Man and the Singer.*

All in the Morning Early (folktale)
pb Alger. *All in the Morning Early.*

Angelo, the Naughty One (modern realistic story)
pb Garrett. *Angelo, the Naughty One.*

The Angry Moon (Indian legend)
pb Sleator. *The Angry Moon.*

Angus and the Ducks (animal story)
Association for Childhood Education International. *Told Under the Blue Umbrella.*
pb Flack. *Angus and the Ducks.*

The Animals' Peace Day (modern imaginative story)
pb Wahl. *The Animals' Peace Day.*

The Armadillo Who Had No Shell (modern imaginative story)
pb Simon. *The Armadillo Who Had No Shell.*

Ask Mr. Bear (animal story)
pb Flack. *Ask Mr. Bear.*
Gruenberg. *Favorite Stories Old and New.*
Huber. *Story and Verse for Children.*

Away Went Wolfgang! (animal story)
pb Kahl. *Away Went Wolfgang!*

3

The Bear's Toothache (modern imaginative story)
pb McPhail. *The Bear's Toothache.*

⤳**Bedtime for Frances** (animal story)
pb Hoban. *Bedtime for Frances.*

The Billy Goat in the Chili Patch (folktale)
pb Lazarus. *The Billy Goat in the Chili Patch.*

⟶**Blueberries for Sal** (modern realistic story)
pb McCloskey. *Blueberries for Sal.*

⟶ **The Boy Who Cried Wolf** (fable)

ALSO CALLED: The Shepherd's Boy; 'Wolf! Wolf!'
⟶Aesop. *Fables from Aesop.*
Aesop. *The Fables of Aesop.*
pb Evans. *The Boy Who Cried Wolf.*

The Bremen Town Musicians (folktale)

ALSO CALLED: The Four Musicians; The Musicians of Bremen;
 The Traveling Musicians
pb Grimm. *The Bremen Town Musicians.*
⟶*pb* Grimm. *The Four Musicians.*
 Grimm. *The House in the Wood.*
 Grimm. *Household Stories.*
 Grimm. *Tales from Grimm.*
pb Grimm. *The Traveling Musicians.*

ALSO CALLED: The Sheep and the Pig That Built the House
 Association for Childhood Education International. *Told Under the Green Umbrella.*
 Wiggin and Smith. *The Fairy Ring.*

PARALLEL: The Animal Musicians (folktale)
 Alegria. *The Three Wishes.*

PARALLEL: Jack and His Comrades (folktale)
 Jacobs. *Celtic Folk and Fairy Tales.*

PARALLEL: Jack and the Friendly Animals (folktale)
 Danaher. *Folktales of the Irish Countryside.*

PARALLEL: Jack and the Robbers (folktale)
 Chase. *The Jack Tales.*

A Bundle of Sticks (fable)
pb Evans. *A Bundle of Sticks.*

The Cat at Night (animal story)
 pb Ipcar. *The Cat at Night.*

Cheese, Peas, and Chocolate Pudding (modern realistic story)
 Sechrist and Woolsey. *It's Time for Story Hour.*

> **The Circus Baby** (animal story)
 pb Petersham. *The Circus Baby.*

> **The Cock, the Mouse, and the Little Red Hen** (folktale)
 Arbuthnot. *Time for Fairy Tales.*
 Hutchinson. *Chimney Corner Stories.*
 pb Lefèvre. *The Cock, the Mouse, and the Little Red Hen.*
 Untermeyer. *Big and Little Creatures.*

> **Corduroy** (toy story)
 pb Freeman. *Corduroy.*

A Crocodile's Tale (folktale)
 pb Aruego. *A Crocodile's Tale.*

Curious George Takes a Job (animal story)
 pb Rey. *Curious George Takes a Job.*

> **Dandelion** (animal story)
 pb Freeman. *Dandelion.*

Down down the Mountain (modern realistic story)
 pb Credle. *Down down the Mountain.*
 Sechrist and Woolsey. *It's Time for Story Hour.*

Drakesbill and His Friends (folktale)

 ALSO CALLED: Drakestail
 Hutchinson. *Fireside Stories.*
 Johnson, Sickels, and Sayers. *Anthology of Children's Literature.*
 Lang. *Red Fairy Book.*
 Perrault. *Favorite Fairy Tales Told in France.*
 Wiggin and Smith. *The Fairy Ring.*

 PARALLEL: Red-Chicken (folktale)
 Duvoisin. *The Three Sneezes.*

Edie Changes Her Mind (modern realistic story)
 pb Johnston. *Edie Changes Her Mind.*

The Elephant and the Bad Baby (animal story)
pb Foulds. *The Elephant and the Bad Baby.*

↗ **The Five Chinese Brothers** (modern imaginative story)
pb Bishop. *The Five Chinese Brothers.*

FOLKTALE VERSION: The Five Queer Brothers
Hollowell. *A Book of Children's Literature.*

↗**The 500 Hats of Bartholomew Cubbins** (modern imaginative story)
Arbuthnot. *Time for Fairy Tales.*
pb Geisel. *The 500 Hats of Bartholomew Cubbins.*

↗**Frederick** (modern imaginative story)
pb Lionni. *Frederick.*

↗ **The Funny Thing** (modern imaginative story)
pb Gág. *The Funny Thing.*

↗ **The Gingerbread Boy** (folktale)
Colwell. *Tell Me a Story.*
Haviland. *The Fairy Tale Treasury.*

PARALLEL: The Bun (folktale)
pb Brown. *The Bun.*
Hutchinson. *Candlelight Stories.*
Ross. *The Buried Treasure.*

PARALLEL: The Gingerbread Man (folktale)
Kramer. *Read-Aloud Nursery Tales.*

PARALLEL: Johnny-Cake (folktale)
Jacobs. *English Folk and Fairy Tales.*
↗ Withers. *I Saw a Rocket Walk a Mile.*

PARALLEL: The Pancake (folktale)
Arbuthnot. *Time for Fairy Tales.*
Association for Childhood Education International. *Told Under the Green Umbrella.*
Johnson, Sickels, and Sayers. *Anthology of Children's Literature.*

↗MODERN VERSION: Journey Cake, Ho! (modern imaginative story)
pb Sawyer. *Journey Cake, Ho!*

MODERN VERSION: The Runaway Sardine (modern imaginative story)
pb Brock. *The Runaway Sardine.*

The Golden Apple (animal story)
pb Bolliger. *The Golden Apple.*

❓ **Good Night, Owl!** (animal story)
pb Hutchins. *Good Night, Owl!*

The Guinea Pig's Tale (animal story)
Cathon and Schmidt. *Perhaps and Perchance.*

The Gunniwolf (animal story)

ALSO CALLED: The Gunny Wolf
Botkin. *A Treasury of American Folklore.*
pb Harper. *The Gunniwolf.*

The Half-Chick (folktale)
Arbuthnot. *Time for Fairy Tales.*
Haviland. *Favorite Fairy Tales Told in Spain.*
Lang. *Green Fairy Book.*

The Happy Lion (animal story)
pb Fatio. *The Happy Lion.*

Harry the Dirty Dog (animal story)
pb Zion. *Harry the Dirty Dog.*

Henny-Penny (folktale)
Arbuthnot. *Time for Fairy Tales.*
Jacobs. *English Folk and Fairy Tales.*
pb Jacobs. *Henny-Penny.* Illustrated by Paul Galdone.
pb Jacobs. *Henny-Penny.* Illustrated by William Stobbs.
Rackham. *The Arthur Rackham Fairy Book.*
Steel. *English Fairy Tales.*

PARALLEL: The End of the World (folktale)
Bowman and Bianco. *Tales from a Finnish Tupa.*

PARALLEL: The Foolish, Timid Rabbit (fable)
Gruenberg. *Favorite Stories Old and New.*
Hutchinson. *Fireside Stories.*
Jātakas. *Jataka Tales.*

PARALLEL: The Story of Chicken-Licken (folktale)

ALSO CALLED: The Folly of Panic
Power. *Bag O' Tales.*
Shedlock. *The Art of the Story-Teller.*

Herschel the Hero (modern realistic story)
pb Hoff. *Herschel the Hero.*

The House That Jack Built (folktale)
pb *The House That Jack Built.*

> **I'm Going on a Bear Hunt** (action story)
pb Sivulich. *I'm Going on a Bear Hunt.*

> **In the Forest** (modern imaginative story)
pb Ets. *In the Forest.*

> **Inch by Inch** (modern imaginative story)
pb Lionni. *Inch by Inch.*

Jenny's Birthday Book (modern imaginative story)
pb Averill. *Jenny's Birthday Book.*

The King of the Birds (animal story)
Cathon and Schmidt. *Perhaps and Perchance.*

The King's Choice (folktale)
pb Shivkumar. *The King's Choice.*

Lengthy (modern imaginative story)
pb Hoff. *Lengthy.*

> **The Lion and the Mouse** (fable)
Aesop. *The Aesop for Children.*
> Aesop. *The Fables of Aesop.*
Arbuthnot. *Time for Fairy Tales.*
Hazeltine. *Children's Stories to Read or Tell.*

PARALLEL: The Lion and the Rat (fable)
pb La Fontaine. *The Lion and the Rat.*

Little Bear (modern imaginative story)
pb Minarik. *Little Bear.*

Little Hatchy Hen (animal story)
pb Flora. *Little Hatchy Hen.*

> **The Little House** (modern realistic story)
pb Burton. *The Little House.*
Johnson, Sickels, and Sayers. *Anthology of Children's Literature.*

⌐ **Little Toot** (modern imaginative story)
   pb Gramatky. *Little Toot.*
   Johnson, Sickels, and Sayers. *Anthology of Children's Literature.*

The Little White Hen (animal story)
   pb Hewett. *The Little White Hen.*

The Lonely Doll (modern imaginative story)
   pb Wright. *The Lonely Doll.*

⌐ **Madeline** (modern realistic story)
   pb Bemelmans. *Madeline.*

The Magic Feather Duster (modern imaginative story)
   pb Lipkind. *The Magic Feather Duster.*

The Magic Lollipop (modern imaginative story)
   pb Koshland. *The Magic Lollipop.*

⌐ **Make Way for Ducklings** (modern realistic story)
   pb McCloskey. *Make Way for Ducklings.*

⌐ **May I Bring a Friend?** (modern imaginative story)
   pb De Regniers. *May I Bring a Friend?*

The Meeting of the Young Mice (folktale)
   Price. *The Rich Man and the Singer.*

   PARALLEL: Belling the Cat (fable)
   Aesop. *The Fables of Aesop.*

⌐ **The Mighty Hunter** (modern imaginative story)
   pb Hader. *The Mighty Hunter.*

⌐ **Mike Mulligan and His Steam Shovel** (modern imaginative story)
   Arbuthnot. *Time for Fairy Tales.*
   pb Burton. *Mike Mulligan and His Steam Shovel.*

⌐ **The Milkmaid and Her Pail** (fable)
   Aesop. *The Aesop for Children.*
   Aesop. *The Fables of Aesop.*
   Sheehan. *A Treasury of Catholic Children's Stories.*

   PARALLEL: The Egg of Fortune (folktale)
   Spicer. *Long Ago in Serbia.*

PARALLEL: The Lad and the Fox (folktale)
Haviland. *Favorite Fairy Tales Told in Sweden.*

MODERN VERSION: Don't Count Your Chicks (modern realistic story)
pb Aulaire, d'. *Don't Count Your Chicks.*

MODERN VERSION: The Maid and Her Pail of Milk (modern realistic story)
pb Evans. *The Maid and Her Pail of Milk.*

Millions of Cats (modern imaginative story)
pb Gág. *Millions of Cats.*
Johnson, Sickels, and Sayers. *Anthology of Children's Literature.*

Mr. Brown and Mr. Gray (modern imaginative story)
pb Wondriska. *Mr. Brown and Mr. Gray.*

Mr. Gumpy's Outing (animal story)
pb Burningham. *Mr. Gumpy's Outing.*

Mr. Vinegar (folktale)
Arbuthnot. *Time for Fairy Tales.*
Hutchinson. *Chimney Corner Stories.*
Jacobs. *English Folk and Fairy Tales.*
Steel. *English Fairy Tales.*

The Mitten (folktale)
pb Tresselt. *The Mitten.*

The Monkeys and the Little Red Hats (folktale)
Carpenter. *African Wonder Tales.*

PARALLEL: Fifty Red Night-Caps (folktale)
Williams-Ellis. *Fairy Tales from the British Isles.*

MODERN VERSION: Caps for Sale (modern imaginative story)
pb Slobodkina. *Caps for Sale.*

Moses in the Bulrushes (Bible story)
Bible—Old Testament. Exodus, chap. 2.
Gruenberg. *Favorite Stories Old and New.*
Petersham. *Moses.*
Worm. *More Stories from the Old Testament.*

The Neighbors (folktale)
pb Brown. *The Neighbors.*

Noah and the Ark (Bible story)

ALSO CALLED: The Flood and Noah's Ark
Bible—Old Testament. Genesis, chaps. 6–8.
Gruenberg. *Favorite Stories Old and New.*
Worm. *Stories from the Old Testament.*

No Room (folktale)
Dobbs. *No Room.*

PARALLEL: A Cow in the House (folktale)
pb Watts. *A Cow in the House.*

PARALLEL: It Could Be Worse (folktale)
pb Chroman. *It Could Be Worse.*

MODERN VERSION: Too Much Noise (animal story)
pb McGovern. *Too Much Noise.*

MODERN VERSION: The Wise Man on the Mountain (modern imaginative
story)
pb Dillon. *The Wise Man on the Mountain.*

The Old Woman and Her Pig (folktale)
Association for Childhood Education International. *Told Under the
Green Umbrella.*
Jacobs. *English Folk and Fairy Tales.*
Mother Goose. *Nursery Rhyme Book.*
pb The Old Woman and Her Pig.
Steel. *English Fairy Tales.*

PARALLEL: The Monkey's Pomegranate (folktale)
Lowe. *The Little Horse of Seven Colors.*

PARALLEL: Nanny Who Wouldn't Go Home to Supper (folktale)
Hutchinson. *Candlelight Stories.*

PARALLEL: The Old Dame and Her Silver Sixpence (folktale)
Power. *Bag O' Tales.*

PARALLEL: The Rooster and the Hen (folktale)
Bowman and Bianco. *Tales from a Finnish Tupa.*

Once a Mouse (fable)
pb Hitopadésa. *Once a Mouse.*

One Fine Day (folktale)
pb Hogrogian. *One Fine Day.*

One Silver Second (folktale)
pb Hogstrom. *One Silver Second.*

The Outside Cat (animal story)
pb Woolley. *The Outside Cat.*

The Owl and the Woodpecker (animal story)
pb Wildsmith. *The Owl and the Woodpecker.*

Pelle's New Suit (modern realistic story)
   Association for Childhood Education International. *Told Under the Blue Umbrella.*
pb Beskow. *Pelle's New Suit.*
   Gruenberg. *Favorite Stories Old and New.*
   Johnson, Sickels, and Sayers. *Anthology of Children's Literature.*

Play with Me (modern realistic story)
pb Ets. *Play with Me.*

The Poppy Seed Cakes (modern imaginative story)
   Association for Childhood Education International. *Told Under the Blue Umbrella.*
   Clark. *The Poppy Seed Cakes.*
   Gruenberg. *Favorite Stories Old and New.*

Prince Bertram the Bad (modern imaginative story)
pb Lobel. *Prince Bertram the Bad.*

Pumpkinseeds (modern realistic story)
pb Yezback. *Pumpkinseeds.*

Rain, Rain Rivers (modern realistic story)
pb Shulevitz. *Rain, Rain Rivers.*

Rosa-Too-Little (modern realistic story)
pb Felt. *Rosa-Too-Little.*

Rosie's Walk (modern imaginative story)
pb Hutchins. *Rosie's Walk.*

The Runaway Bunny (animal story)
pb Brown. *The Runaway Bunny.*

Sam (modern realistic story)
pb Scott. *Sam.*

Smoke (modern realistic story)
  pb Olsen. *Smoke.*

The Snowy Day (modern realistic story)
  pb Keats. *The Snowy Day.*

The So-So Cat (modern imaginative story)
  pb Hurd. *The So-So Cat.*

The Stolen Necklace (folktale)
  pb Rockwell. *The Stolen Necklace.*

The Story About Ping (modern realistic story)
  pb Flack and Wiese. *The Story About Ping.*

The Story of Ferdinand (animal story)
    Gruenberg. *Favorite Stories Old and New.*
  pb Leaf. *The Story of Ferdinand.*

The Story of Pancho and the Bull with the Crooked Tail (modern realistic story)
  pb Hader. *The Story of Pancho and the Bull with the Crooked Tail.*

The Sultan's Bath (folktale)
  pb Ambrus. *The Sultan's Bath.*

Sunflowers for Tina (modern realistic story)
  pb Baldwin. *Sunflowers for Tina.*

The Surprise Party (animal story)
  pb Hutchins. *The Surprise Party.*

The Tale of a Black Cat (action story)
    Johnson. *The Oak-Tree Fairy Book.*

The Tale of Peter Rabbit (modern imaginative story)
    Huber. *Story and Verse for Children.*
    Hutchinson. *Chimney Corner Stories.*
    Johnson, Sickels, and Sayers. *Anthology of Children's Literature.*
  pb Potter. *The Tale of Peter Rabbit.*
    Ward. *Stories to Dramatize.*

⟋ **The Three Bears** (folktale)

ALSO CALLED: The Story of the Three Bears
Brooke. *The Golden Goose Book.*
De La Mare. *Animal Stories.*
Gruenberg. *Favorite Stories Old and New.*
Jacobs. *English Folk and Fairy Tales.*
Lang. *Green Fairy Book.*

➤ **The Three Billy Goats Gruff** (folktale)

ALSO CALLED: The Three Goats
pb Asbjörnsen. *The Three Billy Goats Gruff.* Illustrated by Marcia Brown.
pb Asbjörnsen. *The Three Billy Goats Gruff.* Illustrated by Paul Galdone.
pb Asbjörnsen. *The Three Billy Goats Gruff.* Illustrated by William Stobbs.
Asbjörnsen and Moe. *East of the Sun and West of the Moon.*
Jones. *Scandinavian Legends and Folk-Tales.*

PARALLEL: Sody Sallyraytus (folktale)
Chase. *Grandfather Tales.*

Three Little Animals (modern imaginative story)
pb Brown. *Three Little Animals.*

➤ **The Three Little Pigs** (folktale)

ALSO CALLED: The Story of the Three Little Pigs
Brooke. *The Golden Goose Book.*
Colwell. *Tell Me a Story.*
De La Mare. *Animal Stories.*
Jacobs. *English Folk and Fairy Tales.*
pb The Story of the Three Little Pigs. Illustrated by William Stobbs.

The Three Wishes (folktale)
Jacobs. *More English Folk and Fairy Tales.*
pb Jacobs. *The Three Wishes.* Illustrated by Paul Galdone.
Sechrist and Woolsey. *It's Time for Story Hour.*

PARALLEL: The Old Woman and the Fish (folktale)
Haviland. *Favorite Fairy Tales Told in Sweden.*

PARALLEL: The Three Wishes (folktale)
Dobbs. *Once Upon a Time.*
Gruenberg. *Favorite Stories Old and New.*

PARALLEL: The Three Wishes (folktale)
Jewett. *Which Was Witch?*

PARALLEL: The Three Wishes (folktale)
Ward. *Stories to Dramatize.*

Tico and the Golden Wings (modern imaginative story)
  pb Lionni. *Tico and the Golden Wings.*

Timid Timothy (animal story)
  pb Williams. *Timid Timothy.*

The Tomten (modern imaginative story)
  pb Lindgren. *The Tomten.*

Tot Botot and His Little Flute (modern imaginative story)
  pb Cathon. *Tot Botot and His Little Flute.*

The Town Mouse and the Country Mouse (fable)
  Aesop. *The Fables of Aesop.*
  pb Aesop. *The Town Mouse and the Country Mouse.*
  Association for Childhood Education International. *Told Under the Green Umbrella.*
  Huber. *Story and Verse for Children.*

  MODERN VERSION: The Tale of Johnny Town-Mouse (modern imaginative story)
  pb Potter. *The Tale of Johnny Town-Mouse.*

The Travels of a Fox (folktale)
  Arbuthnot. *Time for Fairy Tales.*
  Association for Childhood Education International. *Told Under the Green Umbrella.*
  Hutchinson. *Chimney Corner Stories.*
  Withers. *I Saw a Rocket Walk a Mile.*

  PARALLEL: Giacco and His Bean (folktale)
  Hardendorff. *Tricky Peik.*

The Turnip (folktale)
  pb Domanska. *The Turnip.*

  VARIANT: The Great Big Enormous Turnip (folktale)
  pb Tolstoi. *The Great Big Enormous Turnip.*

The Twist-Mouth Family (action story)
  Johnson. *The Oak-Tree Fairy Book.*

Wait for William (modern realistic story)
  pb Flack. *Wait for William.*

What's in the Dark? (modern imaginative story)
  pb Memling. *What's in the Dark?*

When the Root Children Wake Up (modern imaginative story)
pb Olfers. *When the Root Children Wake Up.*

➤ **Where the Wild Things Are** (modern imaginative story)
pb Sendak. *Where the Wild Things Are.*

➤ **Whistle for Willie** (modern realistic story)
pb Keats. *Whistle for Willie.*

Who Took the Farmer's Hat? (modern imaginative story)
pb Nodset. *Who Took the Farmer's Hat?*

Why Cats Wash After Meals (folktale)
Nixon. *Animal Legends.*

PARALLEL: Why Cats Always Wash After Eating (folktale)
Hardendorff. *Tricky Peik.*

Why the Jackal Won't Speak to the Hedgehog (folktale)
pb Berson. *Why the Jackal Won't Speak to the Hedgehog.*

➐ **Why the Sun and Moon Live in the Sky** (folktale)
Arnott. *African Myths and Legends.*
pb Dayrell. *Why the Sun and Moon Live in the Sky* (folktale)
Jablow and Withers. *The Man in the Moon.*

Why the Sun Was Late (folktale)
pb Elkin. *Why the Sun Was Late.*

➐ **The Wolf and the Seven Kids** (folktale)

ALSO CALLED: The Wolf and the Seven Goats; The Wolf and the Seven
Little Kids
Grimm. *Fairy Tales.*
Grimm. *Household Stories.*
pb Grimm. *The Wolf and the Seven Little Kids.*

The Wonderful Dragon of Timlin (modern imaginative story)
pb De Paola. *The Wonderful Dragon of Timlin.*

Stories of Special Interest to Children from Six to Ten Years of Age

Ah Mee's Invention (modern imaginative story)
Chrisman. *Shen of the Sea.*
Fenner. *Time to Laugh.*

Aladdin; or, The Wonderful Lamp (folktale)

ALSO CALLED: The Story of Ala-ed-din; or, The Wonderful Lamp
Arabian Nights' Entertainments. *Arabian Nights.* Edited by
Padraic Colum.
Arabian Nights' Entertainments. *Arabian Nights.* Edited by
Andrew Lang.
Arabian Nights' Entertainments. *The Arabian Nights: Their
Best-Known Tales.* Edited by Wiggin and Smith.
Johnson, Sickels, and Sayers. *Anthology of Children's Literature.*
Rackham. *The Arthur Rackham Fairy Book.*

Androcles and the Lion (fable)
pb Aesop. *Androcles and the Lion.*
Aesop. *The Fables of Aesop.*
Baldwin. *Favorite Tales of Long Ago.*
Gruenberg. *Favorite Stories Old and New.*
Untermeyer. *The World's Great Stories.*

PARALLEL: Kindai and the Ape (folktale)
Aardema. *Tales for the Third Ear from Equatorial Africa.*

MODERN VERSION: Andy and the Lion (modern imaginative story)
pb Daugherty. *Andy and the Lion.*

Aniello (folktale)
Manning-Sanders. *A Book of Wizards.*

VARIANT: The Wonderful Stone (folktale)
Hampden. *The House of Cats.*

Baba Yaga and the Little Girl with the Kind Heart (folktale)
ALSO CALLED: Baba Yaga
Fenner. *Giants & Witches and a Dragon or Two.*
Hoke. *Witches, Witches, Witches.*
Ross. *The Lost Half-Hour.*

The Baker's Daughter (modern realistic story)
Bleecker. *Big Music.*
Fenner. *Fools and Funny Fellows.*
Sechrist and Woolsey. *It's Time for Story Hour.*

Baldpate (folktale)
Hampden. *The Gypsy Fiddle.*

Beany and His New Recorder (modern realistic story)
pb Panter. *Beany and His New Recorder.*

The Beautiful Blue Jay (folktale)
Spellman. *The Beautiful Blue Jay.*

Beauty and the Beast (folktale)
Carey. *Fairy Tales of Long Ago.*
Dalgliesh. *The Enchanted Book.*
Lang. *Blue Fairy Book.*
Pearce. *Beauty and the Beast.*
Perrault. *Favorite Fairy Tales Told in France.*
Rackham. *The Arthur Rackham Fairy Book.*

Beetle (folktale)
Sheehan. *Folk and Fairy Tales from Around the World.*

The Bell of Atri (Italian legend)
Baldwin. *Favorite Tales of Long Ago.*
Longfellow. *Poems of Henry Wadsworth Longfellow* (verse).
Olcott. *Story-Telling Poems* (verse).
Untermeyer. *The World's Great Stories.*

Billy Beg and the Bull (folktale)
Adams and Bacon. *A Book of Giant Stories.*
Fenner. *Giants & Witches and a Dragon or Two.*
Haviland. *Favorite Fairy Tales Told in Ireland.*

Hutchinson. *Chimney Corner Fairy Tales.*
Johnson, Sickels, and Sayers. *Anthology of Children's Literature.*
Ross. *The Lost Half-Hour.*

Blabbermouth (folktale)
    Daniels. *The Falcon Under the Hat.*

    VARIANT: The Silly Goose War (folktale)
    Durham. *Tit for Tat.*

Black Magic (folktale)
    Boggs and Davis. *Three Golden Oranges.*

The Blind Man and the Deaf Man (folktale)

    ALSO CALLED: The Blind Man, the Deaf Man, and the Donkey
    Baker. *The Golden Lynx.*
    Haviland. *Favorite Fairy Tales Told in India.*

The Blind Men and the Elephant (fable)
    Baldwin. *Favorite Tales of Long Ago.*
pb Quigley. *The Blind Men and the Elephant.*
pb Saxe. *The Blind Men and the Elephant.*

Boots and His Brothers (folktale)

    ALSO CALLED: Peter, Paul, and Espen Cinderlad
    Arbuthnot. *Time for Fairy Tales.*
    Association for Childhood Education International. *Told Under the Green Umbrella.*
    Huber. *Story and Verse for Children.*
    Hutchinson. *Chimney Corner Fairy Tales.*

    MODERN VERSION: How Boots Befooled the King (modern imaginative story)
    Pyle. *The Wonder Clock.*
    Sechrist and Woolsey. *It's Time for Story Hour.*

The Boy Who Drew Cats (folktale)
    Gruenberg: *Favorite Stories Old and New.*
    Hearn. *The Boy Who Drew Cats.*
    Hearn. *Japanese Fairy Tales.*

The Boy Without a Name (folktale)
    Holding. *The King's Contest.*

The Brave Little Tailor (folktale)

ALSO CALLED: The Gallant Tailor; Seven at a Blow; The Valiant Little
   Tailor; The Valiant Tailor
   Adams and Bacon. *A Book of Giant Stories.*
   Fenner. *Adventure: Rare and Magical.*
   Grimm. *The House in the Wood.*
   Grimm. *The Valiant Little Tailor.*
   Lang. *Blue Fairy Book.*
pb Werth. *The Valiant Tailor.*

PARALLEL: The Cobbler (folktale)
   Lum. *Italian Fairy Tales.*

PARALLEL: Donal O'Ciaran from Connaught (folktale)
   MacManus. *The Bold Heroes of Hungry Hill.*

PARALLEL: Jack and the Varmints (folktale)
   Chase. *The Jack Tales.*

PARALLEL: Nazar the Brave (folktale)
   Tashjian. *Once There Was and Was Not.*

PARALLEL: Sixty at a Blow (folktale)
pb Price. *Sixty at a Blow.*

Budulinek (folktale)
   Fenner. *Adventure: Rare and Magical.*
   Fillmore. *The Shepherd's Nosegay.*
   Ross. *The Lost Half-Hour.*

The Buried Treasure (folktale)
   Ross. *The Buried Treasure.*

The Burning of the Rice Fields (folktale)
   Bryant. *How to Tell Stories to Children.*

VARIANT: The Wave (folktale)
   Hodges. *The Wave.*

Can Men Be Such Fools as All That? (modern imaginative story)
   Farjeon. *The Old Nurse's Stocking-Basket.*

The Cat and the Parrot (folktale)
   Bryant. *How to Tell Stories to Children.*
   Haviland. *Favorite Fairy Tales Told in India.*
   Johnson, Sickels, and Sayers. *Anthology of Children's Literature.*

Ross. *The Lost Half-Hour.*
Sechrist and Woolsey. *It's Time for Story Hour.*
Temple. *Shirley Temple's Storytime Favorites.*

PARALLEL: The Fat Cat (folktale)
pb Kent. *The Fat Cat.*

PARALLEL: Kuratko the Terrible (folktale)
Davis. *A Baker's Dozen.*
Haviland. *Favorite Fairy Tales Told in Czechoslovakia.*

PARALLEL: Slip! Slop! Gobble! (folktale)
pb Hardendorff. *Slip! Slop! Gobble!*

Chanina and the Angels (folktale)
Baker. *The Talking Tree.*

Chanticleer and the Fox (folktale)

ALSO CALLED: Chanticleer
pb Cooney. *Chanticleer and the Fox.*
Untermeyer. *The Firebringer.*

PARALLEL: The Fox and the Crow (fable)
Aesop. *The Fables of Aesop.*

The Child in the Bamboo Grove (folktale)
pb Harris. *The Child in the Bamboo Grove.*

VARIANT: The Princess of Light (folktale)
Uchida. *The Dancing Kettle.*

Chu Cuoi's Trip to the Moon (folktale)
Robertson. *Fairy Tales from Viet Nam.*

Cinderella (folktale)
De La Mare. *Tales Told Again.*
Lang. *Blue Fairy Book.*
pb Perrault. *Cinderella.*
Rackham. *The Arthur Rackham Fairy Book.*

PARALLEL: The Anklet of Jewels (folktale)
Arabian Nights' Entertainments. *The Black Monkey.*

PARALLEL: Ashputtel (folktale)

ALSO CALLED: Aschenputtel
   Child Study Association of America. *Castles and Dragons.*
   De La Mare. *Animal Stories.*
   Grimm. *Grimms' Fairy Tales.* Illustrated by Ulrik Schramm.
   Grimm. *Household Stories.*

PARALLEL: Cap o' Rushes (folktale)
   Jacobs. *English Folk and Fairy Tales.*
   Jacobs. *Favorite Fairy Tales Told in England.*
   Steel. *English Fairy Tales.*

PARALLEL: Catskin (folktale)
   Dalgliesh. *The Enchanted Book.*
   De La Mare. *Animal Stories.*
   Jacobs. *More English Folk and Fairy Tales.*

PARALLEL: Catskins (folktale)
   Chase. *Grandfather Tales.*

PARALLEL: Cenerentola (folktale)
   Lum. *Italian Fairy Tales.*

PARALLEL: The Jeweled Slipper (folktale)
   Graham. *The Beggar in the Blanket.*

PARALLEL: Kari Woodengown (folktale)
   Lang. *Red Fairy Book.*

PARALLEL: The Little Scarred One (folktale)

ALSO CALLED: Little Scar Face (American Indian legend)
   Association for Childhood Education International. *Told Under the Green Umbrella.*
   Sheehan. *Folk and Fairy Tales from Around the World.*

PARALLEL: Nomi and the Magic Fish (folktale)
pb Phumla. *Nomi and the Magic Fish.*

PARALLEL: Vasilisa the Beautiful (folktale)
pb *Vasilisa the Beautiful.*

PARALLEL: Zezolla and the Date-Palm Tree (folktale)
   Toor. *The Golden Carnation.*

The Clever Turtle (folktale)
pb Roche. *The Clever Turtle.*

The Clever Wife (folktale)
   Johnson. *The Oak-Tree Fairy Book.*

A Crumb in His Beard (folktale)
Hampden. *The House of Cats.*

Dance of the Animals (folktale)
pb Belpré. *Dance of the Animals.*
Belpré. *The Tiger and the Rabbit.*

The Dancing Cow (modern imaginative story)
Travers. *Mary Poppins,* pp. 62–79.

Daniel in the Lions' Den (Bible story)

ALSO CALLED: Daniel in the Den of Lions; Daniel, the Brave
Young Captive
Bible—Old Testament. Daniel, chap. 6.
Hurlbut. *Hurlbut's Story of the Bible.*
Worm. *More Stories from the Old Testament.*

Dick Whittington and His Cat (folktale)
pb Brown. *Dick Whittington and His Cat.*
Carey. *Fairy Tales of Long Ago.*
De La Mare. *Tales Told Again.*
Rackham. *The Arthur Rackham Fairy Book.*
Reeves. *English Fables and Fairy Stories.*

PARALLEL: The Priceless Cats (folktale)
Jagendorf. *The Priceless Cats.*

Doctor and Detective Too (folktale)
Hatch. *13 Danish Tales.*

PARALLEL: Doctor Know-It-All (folktale)

ALSO CALLED: Doctor Know All
Fenner. *Fools and Funny Fellows.*
Grimm. *Tales from Grimm.*
Ranke. *Folktales of Germany.*

The Donkey Egg (folktale)
Kelsey. *Once the Hodja.*

PARALLEL: The Horse-Egg (folktale)
Jagendorf. *Noodlehead Stories.*

The Doughnuts (modern realistic story)
McCloskey. *Homer Price,* pp. 50–68.
Smith and Hazeltine. *Just for Fun.*

The Dragon and His Grandmother (folktale)
Fenner. *Giants & Witches and a Dragon or Two.*
Grimm. *Tales from Grimm.*
Lang. *Yellow Fairy Book.*
Manning-Sanders. *A Book of Dragons.*

The Dragon and the Dragoon (modern imaginative story)
Hardendorff. *The Frog's Saddle Horse.*

Dragonmaster (folktale)
Quinn. *The Water Sprite of the Golden Town.*

MODERN VERSION: Peter and the Twelve-Headed Dragon (modern
imaginative story)
pb Reesink. *Peter and the Twelve-Headed Dragon.*

The Dutch Boy and the Dike (Dutch legend)
ALSO CALLED: The Boy Who Stopped the Sea; The Hero of Haarlem;
The Leak in the Dike; The Little Hero of Haarlem
Bryant. *How to Tell Stories to Children.*
Dodge. *Hans Brinker*, pp. 123–26.
Gruenberg. *Favorite Stories Old and New.*
Hodges. *Tell It Again* (verse).
Untermeyer. *The World's Great Stories.*

The Earth Gnome (folktale)
Grimm. *More Tales from Grimm.*

East of the Sun and West of the Moon (folktale)
Asbjörnsen and Moe. *East of the Sun and West of the Moon.*
Baker. *The Talking Tree.*
Dalgliesh. *The Enchanted Book.*
Hutchinson. *Chimney Corner Fairy Tales.*
Lang. *Blue Fairy Book.*
Undset. *True and Untrue.*

PARALLEL: Whitebear Whittington (folktale)
Chase. *Grandfather Tales.*

Ebenezer Never-Could-Sneezer (modern imaginative story)
Fenner. *Time to Laugh.*

8,000 Stones (folktale)
pb Wolkstein. *8,000 Stones.*

VARIANT: How to Weigh an Elephant (fable)
Alexander. *Pebbles from a Broken Jar.*

The Emperor and the Kite (modern imaginative story)
pb Yolen. *The Emperor and the Kite.*

The Emperor's New Clothes (modern imaginative story)
Andersen. *Andersen's Fairy Tales.*
pb Andersen. *The Emperor's New Clothes.*
Andersen. *Fairy Tales.*
Andersen. *It's Perfectly True.*
Fenner. *Time to Laugh.*

FOLKTALE VERSION: The Invisible Silk Robe
Tooze. *The Wonderful Wooden Peacock Flying Machine.*

The Escape of the Animals (folktale)
Pridham. *A Gift from the Heart.*

The False Friend (folktale)
Holding. *The King's Contest.*

The Farmer and the King (folktale)
Price. *The Rich Man and the Singer.*

The Fire Bringer (American Indian legend)
Cathon and Schmidt. *Perhaps and Perchance.*
Hazeltine. *Children's Stories to Read or Tell.*
Hodges. *The Fire Bringer.*

VARIANT: How Animals Brought Fire to Man (American Indian myth)
Fisher. *Stories California Indians Told.*

The Fisherman and His Wife (folktale)
Association for Childhood Education International. *Told Under the Green Umbrella.*
pb Grimm. *The Fisherman and His Wife.*
Grimm. *Tales from Grimm.*
Hutchinson. *Chimney Corner Fairy Tales.*
Lang. *Green Fairy Book.*

PARALLEL: The Golden Fish (folktale)
Ransome. *Old Peter's Russian Tales.*

PARALLEL: The Old Woman Who Lived in a Vinegar Bottle (folktale)
Godden. *The Old Woman Who Lived in a Vinegar Bottle.*

The Fisherman Under the Sea (modern imaginative story)
pb Matsutani. *The Fisherman Under the Sea.*

The Flea (folktale)
    Bleecker. *Big Music.*
    Haviland. *Favorite Fairy Tales Told in Spain.*

The Flying Ship (folktale)

    ALSO CALLED: The Fool of the World and the Flying Ship; The Seven Simeons
pb Artzybasheff. *The Seven Simeons.*
    Association for Childhood Education International. *Told Under the
      Green Umbrella.*
    Frost. *Legends of the United Nations.*
    Haviland. *Favorite Fairy Tales Told in Russia.*
    Lang. *Yellow Fairy Book.*
pb Ransome. *The Fool of the World and the Flying Ship.*
    Ransome. *Old Peter's Russian Tales.*

    PARALLEL: The Seven Simons (folktale)
    Lang. *Crimson Fairy Book.*

    PARALLEL: The Ship That Sailed by Land and Sea (folktale)
    Bowman and Bianco. *Tales from a Finnish Tupa.*

The Forest Bride (folktale)

    ALSO CALLED: The Mouse Bride
    Bowman and Bianco. *Tales from a Finnish Tupa.*
    Fenner. *Princesses & Peasant Boys.*
    Fillmore. *The Shepherd's Nosegay.*
    Provensen. *The Provensen Book of Fairy Tales.*

    PARALLEL: The Mouse-Princess (folktale)
    Picard. *French Legends, Tales, and Fairy Stories.*

    MODERN VERSION: The White Cat (modern imaginative story)
    Aulnoy. *The White Cat.*
    Dalgliesh. *The Enchanted Book.*
    Lang. *Blue Fairy Book.*
    Wiggin and Smith. *The Fairy Ring.*

The Forty Thieves (folktale)

    ALSO CALLED: Ali Baba and the Forty Thieves
    Arabian Nights' Entertainments. *The Arabian Nights.* Edited by
      Padraic Colum

Arabian Nights' Entertainments. *Arabian Nights.* Edited by Andrew Lang
Arabian Nights' Entertainments. *The Arabian Nights: Their Best-Known Tales.* Edited by Wiggin and Smith.

The Frog Prince (folktale)
Dalgliesh. *The Enchanted Book.*
Grimm. *Household Stories.*

PARALLEL: The Well o' the World's End (folktale)
Jacobs. *English Folk and Fairy Tales.*
Reeves. *English Fables and Fairy Stories.*

From Tiger to Anansi (folktale)
Sherlock. *Anansi, the Spider Man.*

VARIANT: Tiger Story, Anansi Story (folktale)
Sherlock. *West Indian Folk-Tales.*

The Funny Little Woman (folktale)
pb Mosel. *The Funny Little Woman.*

VARIANT: The Old Woman and Her Dumpling (folktale)
Hearn. *Japanese Fairy Tales.*

Gears and Gasoline (modern imaginative story)
Fenner. *Adventure: Rare and Magical.*

The Ghost Who Was Afraid of Being Bagged (folktale)
Hardendorff. *Just One More.*

The Giant and the Dwarf (folktale)
Hardendorff. *Just One More.*

The Giant and the Rabbit (folktale)
Lyons. *Tales the People Tell in Mexico.*

The Giant Who Had No Heart in His Body (folktale)
Adams and Bacon. *A Book of Giant Stories.*
Asbjörnsen and Moe. *East of the Sun and West of the Moon.*
Fenner. *Giants & Witches and a Dragon or Two.*
Jones. *Scandinavian Legends and Folk-Tales.*
Undset. *True and Untrue.*

PARALLEL: The Crochera (folktale)
MacManus. *The Bold Heroes of Hungry Hill.*

A Gift from the Heart (folktale)
Pridham. *A Gift from the Heart.*

The Girl and the Goatherd (modern imaginative story)
pb Ness. *The Girl and the Goatherd.*

The Girl Monkey and the String of Pearls (fable)
Jàtakas. *More Jataka Tales.*
VARIANT: The Stolen Necklace (fable)
pb Rockwell. *The Stolen Necklace.*

The Girl Who Could Think (folktale)
Gruenberg. *Favorite Stories Old and New.*

The Goat Well (folktale)
Colwell. *A Second Storyteller's Choice.*
Courlander and Leslau. *The Fire on the Mountain.*

The Golden Goose (folktale)
Brooke. *The Golden Goose Book.*
pb Grimm. *The Golden Goose.*
Grimm. *Household Stories.*
Johnson, Sickels, and Sayers. *Anthology of Children's Literature.*
Lang. *Red Fairy Book.*
Lines. *Nursery Stories.*
PARALLEL: The Lamb with the Golden Fleece (folktale)
Thompson. *One Hundred Favorite Folk Tales.*

The Golden Gourd (folktale)
Carpenter. *South American Wonder Tales.*

The Golden Lynx (folktale)
Baker. *The Golden Lynx.*

The Golden Touch (Greek myth)
ALSO CALLED: The Golden Touch of King Midas; Midas
Benson. *Stories of the Gods and Heroes.*
Coolidge. *Greek Myths.*
Hawthorne. *The Golden Touch.*
Hawthorne. *A Wonder Book and Tanglewood Tales.*
Untermeyer. *The Firebringer.*

Grandmother Marta (folktale)
Pridham. *A Gift from the Heart.*

The Grateful Beasts (folktale)
Carpenter. *The Elephant's Bathtub.*

The Great Quillow (modern imaginative story)
Thurber. *The Great Quillow.*

Gudbrand on the Hillside (folktale)
Arbuthnot. *Time for Fairy Tales.*
Fenner. *Time to Laugh.*
Smith. *Laughing Matter.*

PARALLEL: Hans in Luck (folktale)
Grimm. *Household Stories.*
Hutchinson. *Fireside Stories.*

PARALLEL: Happy-Go-Lucky (folktale)
pb Wiesner. *Happy-Go-Lucky.*

MODERN VERSION: What the Good Man Does Is Sure to Be Right
(modern imaginative story)

ALSO CALLED: What the Good Man Does Is Always Right
Andersen. *Andersen's Fairy Tales.*
Andersen. *Fairy Tales.*
pb Andersen. *What the Good Man Does Is Always Right.*
Bleecker. *Big Music.*
Rackham. *The Arthur Rackham Fairy Book.*
Watson. *Tales for Telling.*

A Guest for Halil (folktale)
Kelsey. *Once the Hodja.*

PARALLEL: King Clothes (folktale)
Jagendorf. *The Priceless Cats.*

The Gypsy Fiddle (folktale)
Hampden. *The Gypsy Fiddle.*

Hansel and Gretel (folktale)

ALSO CALLED: Nibble Nibble Mousekin
Grimm. *Fairy Tales.* Illustrated by Ulrik Schramm.
Grimm. *Favorite Fairy Tales Told in Germany.*
pb Grimm. *Hansel and Gretel.*

Grimm. *Household Stories.*
pb Grimm. *Nibble Nibble Mousekin.*
Lang. *Blue Fairy Book.*

The Hare and the Hedgehog (folktale)

ALSO CALLED: The Race Between Hare and Hedgehog
De La Mare. *Animal Stories.*
De La Mare. *Tales Told Again.*
Hutchinson. *Fireside Stories.*
Johnson, Sickels, and Sayers. *Anthology of Children's Literature.*

Hereafterthis (folktale)
Jacobs. *More English Folk and Fairy Tales.*

PARALLEL: Presentneed, Bymeby, and Hereafter (folktale)
Chase. *Grandfather Tales.*

PARALLEL: Shrovetide (folktale)
Tashjian. *Once There Was and Was Not.*

How a Poor Man Was Rewarded (folktale)
Savory. *Lion Outwitted by Hare.*

How Many Donkeys? (folktale)
Kelsey. *Once the Hodja.*

How Spider Got a Thin Waist (folktale)
Arkhurst. *The Adventures of Spider.*

How the Camel Got His Hump (modern imaginative story)
Johnson, Sickels, and Sayers. *Anthology of Children's Literature.*
Kipling. *Just So Stories.*

How the Camel Got His Proud Look (folktale)
Ross. *The Buried Treasure.*

How the Dog Became the Servant of Man (folktale)
Nixon. *Animal Legends.*

How the Hare Told the Truth About His Horse (folktale)
pb Walker. *How the Hare Told the Truth About His Horse.*

How the Manx Cat Lost Its Tail (folktale)
De La Mare. *Animal Stories.*
Young. *How the Manx Cat Lost Its Tail.*

How the Porcupine Outwitted the Fox (folktale)
Barlow. *Latin American Tales from the Pampas to the Pyramids of Mexico.*

How the Robin's Breast Became Red (folktale)

ALSO CALLED: Why the Robin Has a Red Breast
Bailey and Lewis. *Favorite Stories for the Children's Hour.*
Cathon and Schmidt. *Perhaps and Perchance.*
Colwell. *Tell Me Another Story.*

How the Siamese Cats Got the Kink in the End of Their Tails (folktale)
Nixon. *Animal Legends.*

Hudden and Dudden and Donald O'Neary (folktale)
Bleecker. *Big Music.*
Fenner. *Adventure: Rare and Magical.*
Jacobs. *Celtic Folk and Fairy Tales.*
pb Jacobs. *Hudden and Dudden and Donald O'Neary.*

PARALLEL: Jack and the Flock of Sheep (folktale)
Protter. *Gypsy Tales.*

Hungry Spider and the Turtle (folktale)
Courlander and Herzog. *The Cow-Tail Switch.*

The Husband Who Was to Mind the House (folktale)
Arbuthnot. *Time for Fairy Tales.*
Asbjörnsen and Moe. *East of the Sun and West of the Moon.*
Hutchinson. *Candlelight Stories.*

PARALLEL: Gone Is Gone (folktale)
pb Gág. *Gone Is Gone.*
Johnson, Sickels, and Sayers. *Anthology of Children's Literature.*

PARALLEL: How the Peasant Kept House (folktale)
Daniels. *The Falcon Under the Hat.*

PARALLEL: The Husband Who Wanted to Mind the House (folktale)
Price. *The Rich Man and the Singer.*

PARALLEL: When the Husband Stayed Home (folktale)
Savory. *Lion Outwitted by Hare.*

I Am Your Misfortune (folktale)
pb Rudolph. *I Am Your Misfortune.*

MODERN VERSION: How One Turned His Trouble to Some Account
(modern imaginative story)
Pyle. *The Wonder Clock.*

I Know an Old Lady (ballad story)

ALSO CALLED: The Little Old Lady Who Swallowed a Fly
Emrich. *An Almanac of American Folklore.*
pb Miller. *I Know an Old Lady.*

The Ifrit and the Magic Gifts (folktale)
Walker. *The Ifrit and the Magic Gifts.*

Ittki Pittki (modern imaginative story)
pb Chaikin. *Ittki Pittki.*

Jack and the Beanstalk (folktale)
pb *Jack and the Beanstalk.*
  Jacobs. *English Folk and Fairy Tales.*
  Lang. *Red Fairy Book.*
  Rackham. *The Arthur Rackham Fairy Book.*
  Steel. *English Fairy Tales.*

  PARALLEL: Jack and the Bean Tree (folktale)
  Chase. *The Jack Tales.*

The Jackal and the Alligator (folktale)

ALSO CALLED: The Alligator and the Jackal; The Little Alligator and the Jackal
Fenner. *Fools and Funny Fellows.*
Hutchinson. *Fireside Stories.*
Sechrist and Woolsey. *It's Time for Story Hour.*

Jimmy Takes Vanishing Lessons (modern imaginative story)
Brooks. *Jimmy Takes Vanishing Lessons.*
Hitchcock. *Alfred Hitchcock's Haunted Houseful.*

Joco and the Fishbone (folktale)
pb Wiesner. *Joco and the Fishbone.*

Johnny Appleseed (North American legend)
Bailey and Lewis. *Favorite Stories for the Children's Hour.*
Frost. *Legends of the United Nations.*
Le Sueur. *Little Brother of the Wilderness.*
Malcolmson. *Yankee Doodle's Cousins.*
Suddeth and Morenus. *Tales of the Western World.*

The Jolly Tailor Who Became King (folktale)
Bleecker. *Big Music.*
Borski and Miller. *The Jolly Tailor.*

Colwell. *A Storyteller's Choice.*
Haviland. *Favorite Fairy Tales Told in Poland.*

Joseph and His Brothers (Bible story)
Bible—Old Testament. Genesis, chaps. 37, 39–47.
Bowie. *The Bible Story for Boys and Girls.*
Gruenberg. *Favorite Stories Old and New.*
Petersham. *Joseph and His Brothers.*

The King and the Shepherd (folktale)
Tashjian. *Three Apples Fell from Heaven.*

King John and the Abbot of Canterbury (ballad story)
Baldwin. *Favorite Tales of Long Ago.*
Jacobs. *More English Folk and Fairy Tales.*
Untermeyer. *The World's Great Stories.*

PARALLEL: The Gardener, the Abbot, and the King (folktale)
Mehdevi. *Bungling Pedro.*

PARALLEL: The Parson and the Clerk (folktale)
Undset. *True and Untrue.*

King Solomon's Carpet (Jewish legend)

ALSO CALLED: Namalah and the Magic Carpet
Baker. *The Talking Tree.*
Freehof. *Stories of King Solomon.*

King Stork (modern imaginative story)
pb Pyle. *King Stork.*
Pyle. *The Wonder Clock.*
Ross. *The Lost Half-Hour.*

The King's Rijstepap (folktale)
Sechrist and Woolsey. *It's Time for Story Hour.*
Smith. *Laughing Matter.*

Kojata (folktale)
Manning-Sanders. *A Book of Wizards.*

The Lad Who Went to the North Wind (folktale)
Asbjörnsen and Moe. *East of the Sun and West of the Moon.*
Association for Childhood Education International. *Told Under the Green Umbrella.*
Haviland. *Favorite Fairy Tales Told in Norway.*
Hutchinson. *Chimney Corner Fairy Tales.*

PARALLEL: The Donkey Which Made Gold (folktale)
Hampden. *The House of Cats.*

PARALLEL: Jack and the North West Wind (folktale)
Chase. *The Jack Tales.*

PARALLEL: Keloğlan and the Ooh-Genie (folktale)
Walker. *Once There Was and Twice There Wasn't.*

PARALLEL: Per and the North Wind (folktale)
Hardendorff. *Tricky Peik.*

PARALLEL: The Three Gifts (folktale)
Chang. *Tales from Old China.*

PARALLEL: The Wishing Table, the Gold Donkey, and the Cudgel-in-the-Sack
(folktale)
Grimm. *More Tales from Grimm.*

The Laughing Prince (modern imaginative story)
Fenner. *Time to Laugh.*

Lazy Jack (folktale)
Huber. *Story and Verse for Children.*
Hutchinson. *Chimney Corner Tales.*
Jacobs. *English Folk and Fairy Tales.*
Sechrist and Woolsey. *It's Time for Story Hour.*
Steel. *English Fairy Tales.*
pb Werth. *Lazy Jack.*

PARALLEL: The Mixed-up Feet and the Silly Bridegroom (folktale)
Singer. *Zlateh the Goat.*

PARALLEL: Pedro de Malas Artes, or, Clumsy Pedro (folktale)
Lowe. *The Little Horse of Seven Colors.*

PARALLEL: Prudent Hans (folktale)

ALSO CALLED: Goose Hans
Grimm. *Household Stories.*
Grimm. *Three Gay Tales.*

PARALLEL: Silly Jean (folktale)
Duvoisin. *The Three Sneezes.*

PARALLEL: Tony Di-Moany (folktale)
Mehdevi. *Bungling Pedro.*

Lazy Tok (folktale)
Colwell. *A Storyteller's Choice.* *

The Legend of the Orange Princess (folktale)
pb Gobhai. *The Legend of the Orange Princess.*

The Legs of the Moon (folktale)
pb Jacobs. *The Legs of the Moon.*

The Little Rooster and the Turkish Sultan (folktale)

ALSO CALLED: The Little Rooster and the Diamond Button; The Little
Rooster, the Diamond Button, and the Turkish Sultan
Colwell. *Tell Me Another Story.*
Gruenberg. *Favorite Stories Old and New.*
Ross. *The Lost Half-Hour.*
Seredy. *The Good Master,* pp. 129–35.

PARALLEL: The Magical Crock (folktale)
Zajdler. *Polish Fairy Tales.*

VARIANT: The Little Cockerel (folktale)
pb Ambrus. *The Little Cockerel.*

PARALLEL: Pancakes and Pies (folktale)
Manning-Sanders. *A Book of Charms and Changelings.*

Living in W'ales (modern imaginative story)
Association for Childhood Education International. *Told Under the
Magic Umbrella.*
Hughes. *The Spider's Palace.*

The Lorax (modern imaginative story)
pb Geisel. *The Lorax.*

Ma Lien and the Magic Brush (folktale)

ALSO CALLED: Ma Liang and His Magic Brush
pb Kimishima. *Ma Lien and the Magic Brush.*
Wyndham. *Tales the People Tell in China.*

Madam Crab Loses Her Head (folktale)
McDowell. *Third World Voices for Children.*

The Magic Bottles (folktale)
Spellman. *The Beautiful Blue Jay.*

PARALLEL: The Two Bottles (folktale)
Pilkington. *Shamrock and Spear.*

MODERN VERSION: Clever Peter and the Two Bottles (modern imaginative story)
Fenner. *Princesses & Peasant Boys.*
Pyle. *Pepper & Salt.*

The Magic Tree (folktale)
pb McDermott. *The Magic Tree.*

Mammo the Fool (folktale)
Price. *The Rich Man and the Singer.*

The Man Who Lost His Head (modern imaginative story)
pb Bishop. *The Man Who Lost His Head.*

Many Moons (modern imaginative story)
Johnson. *The Princesses.*
Johnson, Sickels, and Sayers. *Anthology of Children's Literature.*
pb Thurber. *Many Moons.*

Master of All Masters (folktale)
Arbuthnot. *Time for Fairy Tales.*
Fenner. *Feasts and Frolics.*
Hutchinson. *Candlelight Stories.*
Jacobs. *English Folk and Fairy Tales.*

Mirza and the Ghul (folktale)
Spicer. *The Kneeling Tree.*

Mr. Rabbit and Mr. Bear (folktale)
Lester. *The Knee-High Man.*

Molly Whuppie (folktale)

ALSO CALLED: Molly Whipple
Adams and Bacon. *A Book of Giant Stories.*
De La Mare. *Tales Told Again.*
Jacobs. *English Folk and Fairy Tales.*
Jacobs. *Favorite Fairy Tales Told in England.*
Reeves. *English Fables and Fairy Stories.*
Steel. *English Fairy Tales.*

PARALLEL: Molly and the Giant (folktale)
pb Werth. *Molly and the Giant.*

PARALLEL: The Mop Servant (folktale)
Pilkington. *Shamrock and Spear.*

The Monastery of No Cares (folktale)
Daniels. *The Falcon Under the Hat.*

The Monkey and the Crocodile (fable)
pb Galdone. *The Monkey and the Crocodile.*

The Moon Princess (folktale)
Spellman. *The Beautiful Blue Jay.*

Moses Delivers the People of Israel (Bible story)
Bible—Old Testament. Exodus, chaps. 7–14.
Bowie. *The Bible Story for Boys and Girls.*
Petersham. *Moses.*
Sherman and Kent. *The Children's Bible.*

The Mysterious Gold and Purple Box (modern realistic story)
Watson. *The Mysterious Gold and Purple Box.*

Nanabozho and the Wild Geese (American Indian legend)
Reid. *Tales of Nanabozho.*

The Ogre, the Sun, and the Raven (folktale)
Manning-Sanders. *A Book of Charms and Changelings.*

Old Acquaintance Is Soon Forgot! (folktale)
Karrick. *Still More Russian Picture Tales.*

Old One-Eye (folktale)
Chase. *Grandfather Tales.*

One-Eye, Two-Eyes, and Three-Eyes (folktale)
ALSO CALLED: Little One-Eye, Little Two-Eyes, and Little Three-Eyes
Arbuthnot. *Time for Fairy Tales.*
Grimm. *Grimms' Fairy Tales.* Illustrated by Arnold Roth.
Hutchinson. *Chimney Corner Fairy Tales.*

One for the Price of Two (folktale)
Jameson. *One for the Price of Two.*

The One Who Wasn't Afraid (folktale)
Deutsch and Yarmolinsky. *Tales of Faraway Folk.*

Oté (folktale)
pb Belpré. *Oté.*

Otto and the Magic Potatoes (animal story)
pb Du Bois. *Otto and the Magic Potatoes.*

The Parrot of Limo Verde (folktale)
Baker. *The Talking Tree.*

The Partnership of Rabbit and Elephant, and What Came of It (folktale)
Fitzgerald. *World Tales for Creative Dramatics and Storytelling.*

Pecos Bill (North American legend)

ALSO CALLED: How Pecos Bill Won and Lost His Bouncing Bride
Bowman. *Pecos Bill.*
Carmer. *Hurricane's Children.*
Malcolmson. *Yankee Doodle's Cousins.*
Peck. *Pecos Bill and Lightning.*

Peter and the Wolf (folktale)
pb Prokofiev. *Peter and the Wolf.*

Peter Ox (folktale)
Hatch. *More Danish Tales.*

The Pied Piper of Hamelin (German legend)

ALSO CALLED: The Ratcatcher of Hamelin
pb Browning. *The Pied Piper of Hamelin* (verse)
Bryant. *How to Tell Stories to Children.*
Lang. *Red Fairy Book.*
Picard. *German Hero-Sagas and Folk-Tales.*
Untermeyer. *The World's Great Stories.*

PARALLEL: The Pied Piper of Franchville (folktale)

ALSO CALLED: The Pied Piper
Jacobs. *More English Folk and Fairy Tales.*
Jacobs. *The Pied Piper.*

The Plain Princess (modern imaginative story)
Arbuthnot. *Time for Fairy Tales.*
Gagliardo. *Let's Read Aloud.*
McGinley. *The Plain Princess.*

Prince Loaf (folktale)
Manning-Sanders. *A Book of Giants.*

The Princess and the Pea (modern imaginative story)
ALSO CALLED: How to Tell a Real Princess; The Real Princess
Andersen. *Andersen's Fairy Tales.*
Andersen. *It's Perfectly True.*
Fenner. *Princesses & Peasant Boys.*
Johnson, Sickels, and Sayers. *Anthology of Children's Literature.*
Shedlock. *The Art of the Story-Teller.*

The Princess of the Mountain (folktale)
Sheehan. *Folk and Fairy Tales from Around the World.*

The Princess of the Rice Fields (folktale)
pb Kimishima. *The Princess of the Rice Fields.*

The Princess on the Glass Hill (folktale)
Asbjörnsen and Moe. *East of the Sun and West of the Moon.*
Association for Childhood Education International. *Told Under the Green Umbrella.*
Baker. *The Talking Tree.*
Fenner. *Princesses & Peasant Boys.*
Haviland. *Favorite Fairy Tales Told in Norway.*
Lang. *Blue Fairy Book.*
Watson. *Tales for Telling.*

PARALLEL: The Princess on the Glass Mountain (folktale)
Durham. *Tit for Tat.*

The Princess Who Could Not Cry (modern imaginative story)
Adams and Bacon. *A Book of Princess Stories.*

The Princess Whom No One Could Silence (folktale)
Dobbs. *Once Upon a Time.*
Gruenberg. *Favorite Stories Old and New.*

Puss in Boots (folktale)
Carey. *Fairy Tales of Long Ago.*
Lang. *Blue Fairy Book.*
pb Perrault. *Puss in Boots.* Illustrated by Marcia Brown.
pb Perrault. *Puss in Boots.* Illustrated by Hans Fischer.

PARALLEL: Mighty Mikko (folktale)

ALSO CALLED: The Beggar Boy and the Fox
  Davis. *A Baker's Dozen.*
  Fenner. *Princesses & Peasant Boys.*
  Fillmore. *The Shepherd's Nosegay.*
  Lang. *Crimson Fairy Book.*

  PARALLEL: The Miller-King (folktale)
  Tashjian. *Once There Was and Was Not.*

  PARALLEL: The Orange Tree King (folktale)
  Chang. *Tales from Old China.*

The Quarrel (folktale)
  Sherlock. *Anansi, the Spider Man.*

Rags-and-Tatters (folktale)
  Baker. *The Golden Lynx.*

Rapunzel (folktale)
  De La Mare. *Tales Told Again.*
  Grimm. *Favorite Fairy Tales Told in Germany.*
  Grimm. *Tales from Grimm.*
  Hoke. *Witches, Witches, Witches.*
  Lang. *Red Fairy Book.*

The Rat-Catcher's Daughter (modern imaginative story)
  Davis. *A Baker's Dozen.*
  Ross. *The Blue Rose.*

Richard Brown and the Dragon (modern imaginative story)
  Bright. *Richard Brown and the Dragon.*

The Ring in the Prairie (Indian legend)
  pb Schoolcraft. *The Ring in the Prairie.*

The Rolling Rice Ball (modern imaginative story)
  pb Yoda. *The Rolling Rice Ball.*

Rumpelstiltskin (folktale)
  De La Mare. *Tales Told Again.*
  Grimm. *Household Stories.*
  pb Grimm. *Rumpelstiltskin.*
  Lang. *Blue Fairy Book.*

  PARALLEL: Tom Tit Tot (folktale)
  Hutchinson. *Chimney Corner Fairy Tales.*

Jacobs. *English Folk and Fairy Tales.*
Jacobs. *The Pied Piper.*
Sechrist and Woolsey. *It's Time for Story Hour.*
Steel. *English Fairy Tales.*
pb *Tom Tit Tot.*

PARALLEL: Whippety Stourie (folktale)
Wilson. *Scottish Folk-Tales and Legends.*

PARALLEL: The White Hen (folktale)
MacManus. *The Bold Heroes of Hungry Hill.*

The Sack of Truth (folktale)
Sechrist and Woolsey. *It's Time for Story Hour.*

PARALLEL: Jesper Who Herded the Hares (folktale)
Lang. *Violet Fairy Book.*

The Sacred Amulet (folktale)
Barlow. *Latin American Tales from the Pampas to the Pyramids of Mexico.*

Saint Francis and the Wolf (Italian legend)

ALSO CALLED: The Truce of the Wolf; The Wolf of Gubbio
Fenner. *Feasts and Frolics.*
Jauss. *Legends of Saints and Beasts.*
pb Politi. *Saint Francis and the Animals.*

Salt (folktale)
pb Afanasev. *Salt.*
Colwell. *A Second Storyteller's Choice.*
Ransome. *Old Peter's Russian Tales.*

The Search for the Magic Lake (folktale)
Barlow. *Latin American Tales from the Pampas to the Pyramids of Mexico.*

The Seven-Year Blessing (folktale)
Spicer. *The Kneeling Tree.*

The Silver Penny (folktale)
Manning-Sanders. *A Book of Wizards.*

The Sleeping Beauty (folktale)
Association for Childhood Education International. *Told Under the Green Umbrella.*
De La Mare. *Tales Told Again.*

Fenner. *Princesses & Peasant Boys.*
pb Grimm. *The Sleeping Beauty.*
Lang. *Blue Fairy Book.*

PARALLEL: Briar Rose (folktale)

ALSO CALLED: Thorn Rose
Grimm. *More Tales from Grimm.*
Hutchinson. *Chimney Corner Fairy Tales.*

MODERN VERSION: Little Daylight (modern imaginative story)
Adams and Bacon. *A Book of Princess Stories.*
Green. *Modern Fairy Stories.*

Sneezy Snatcher and Sammy Small (folktale)
Manning-Sanders. *A Book of Giants.*

The Snow Maiden (folktale)

ALSO CALLED: Snegourka, the Snow Maiden; Snowflake
Gruenberg. *Favorite Stories Old and New.*
Haviland. *Favorite Fairy Tales Told in Russia.*
Ross. *The Buried Treasure.*

Snow White and the Seven Dwarfs (folktale)

ALSO CALLED: Snow drop
De La Mare. *Tales Told Again.*
Grimm. *Household Stories.*
Grimm. *Snow White and the Seven Dwarfs.*
pb Grimm. *Snow-White and the Seven Dwarfs.*
Lang. *Red Fairy Book.*

Soap, Soap, Soap! (folktale)
Chase. *Grandfather Tales.*

The Sorcerer's Apprentice (folktale)
Child Study Association of America. *Castles and Dragons.*
Grimm. *More Tales from Grimm.*
Hosier. *The Sorcerer's Apprentice.*
Johnson, Sickels, and Sayers. *Anthology of Children's Literature.*

The Squire's Bride (folktale)

ALSO CALLED: The Mare at the Wedding
Asbjörnsen and Moe. *Norwegian Folk Tales.*
Carpenter. *Wonder Tales of Horses and Heroes.*
Frost. *Legends of the United Nations.*
Smith. *Laughing Matter.*

The Steadfast Tin Soldier (modern imaginative story)

ALSO CALLED: The Hardy Tin Soldier
Andersen. *Andersen's Fairy Tales.*
Andersen. *It's Perfectly True.*
pb Andersen. *The Steadfast Tin Soldier.*
Johnson, Sickels, and Sayers. *Anthology of Children's Literature.*
Watson. *Tales for Telling.*

Stone Soup (folktale)
pb Brown. *Stone Soup.*

PARALLEL: The Old Woman and the Tramp (folktale)

ALSO CALLED: Nail Soup
Haviland. *Favorite Fairy Tales Told in Sweden.*
Sechrist and Woolsey. *It's Time for Story Hour.*
Smith. *Laughing Matter.*
pb Zemach. *Nail Soup.*

A Story, a Story (folktale)
pb Haley. *A Story, a Story.*

The Storyteller (folktale)
Courlander and Leslau. *The Fire on the Mountain.*

PARALLEL: The Endless Tale (folktale)
Baldwin. *Favorite Tales of Long Ago.*

The Talking Cat (modern realistic story)
Carlson. *The Talking Cat.*

Tamara and the Sea Witch (folktale)
pb Turska. *Tamara and the Sea Witch.*

The Tears of the Dragon (modern imaginative story)
pb Hamada. *The Tears of the Dragon.*

Tengu's Magic Nose Fan (folktale)
Uchida. *The Sea of Gold.*

The Terrible Leak (folktale)
Uchida. *The Magic Listening Cap.*

Three Gold Pieces (folktale)
pb Brandenberg. *Three Gold Pieces.*

The Three Golden Hairs (folktale)
  Fillmore. *The Shepherd's Nosegay.*

  PARALLEL: The Three Golden Hairs of the King of the Cave Giants (folktale)
  Manning-Sanders. *A Book of Giants.*

Three Golden Oranges (folktale)
  Boggs and Davis. *Three Golden Oranges.*

  PARALLEL: The Three Oranges (folktale)
  Picard. *French Legends, Tales, and Fairy Stories.*

The Three Little Pigs and the Ogre (modern imaginative story)
  Pyle. *The Wonder Clock.*

The Three Sillies (folktale)
  De La Mare. *Tales Told Again.*
  Jacobs. *English Folk and Fairy Tales.*
  Sechrist and Woolsey. *It's Time for Story Hour.*
  Steel. *English Fairy Tales.*
  Williams-Ellis. *Fairy Tales from the British Isles.*
  pb Zemach. *The Three Sillies.*

The Three Sneezes (folktale)
  Duvoisin. *The Three Sneezes.*
  Fenner. *Fools and Funny Fellows.*

The Tiger, the Brahman, and the Jackal (folktale)
  ALSO CALLED: The Brahman, the Tiger, and the Six Judges
  Arbuthnot. *Time for Fairy Tales.*
  Bleecker. *Big Music.*
  Haviland. *Favorite Fairy Tales Told in India.*
  Johnson, Sickels, and Sayers. *Anthology of Children's Literature.*
  pb Steel. *The Tiger, the Brahman, and the Jackal.*
  Wiggin and Smith. *The Fairy Ring.*

  PARALLEL: As the World Pays (folktale)
  Zajdler. *Polish Fairy Tales.*

  PARALLEL: Master Kho and the Tiger (folktale)
  Brockett. *Burmese and Thai Folk Tales.*

  PARALLEL: The Ungrateful Tiger (folktale)
  Carpenter. *The Elephant's Bathtub.*

Tikki Tikki Tembo (folktale)

ALSO CALLED: Tiki-Tiki-Tembo
Hardendorff. *The Frog's Saddle Horse.*
pb Mosel. *Tikki Tikki Tembo.*

The Tinder Box (modern imaginative story)
Andersen. *Andersen's Fairy Tales.*
Andersen. *Fairy Tales.*
Andersen. *It's Perfectly True.*
Dalgliesh. *The Enchanted Book.*
Fenner. *Adventure: Rare and Magical.*
Lang. *Yellow Fairy Book.*

Ting-a-ling's Visit to Turilira (modern imaginative story)
Bleecker. *Big Music.*
Davis. *A Baker's Dozen.*
Stockton. *Ting-a-ling Tales.*

Toads and Diamonds (folktale)
Lang. *Blue Fairy Book.*
Rackham. *The Arthur Rackham Fairy Book.*

Tom Thumb (folktale)
Brooke. *The Golden Goose Book.*
pb *The Diverting Adventures of Tom Thumb.*
pb Grimm. *Tom Thumb.*
Jacobs. *English Folk and Fairy Tales.*
Jacobs. *Favorite Fairy Tales Told in England.*
Reeves. *English Fables and Fairy Stories.*

PARALLEL: Issun Boshi, the Inchling (folktale)
Ishii. *Issun Boshi, the Inchling.*

A Tug of War (folktale)
Fitzgerald. *World Tales for Creative Dramatics and Storytelling.*

VARIANT: The Extraordinary Tug-of-War (folktale)
pb Schatz. *The Extraordinary Tug-of-War.*

PARALLEL: The Tug of War (folktale)
Hurlong. *Adventures of Jabotí on the Amazon.*

The Turtle Who Couldn't Stop Talking (fable)

ALSO CALLED: The Talkative Tortoise
Gruenberg. *Favorite Stories Old and New.*
Jātakas. *Jataka Tales.*
Power. *Bag O' Tales.*

VARIANT: Look, There Is a Turtle Flying (folktale)
pb Domanska. *Look, There Is a Turtle Flying.*

PARALLEL: The Tortoise Talked (folktale)
Chang. *Chinese Fairy Tales.*

The Twelve Dancing Princesses (folktale)
Dalgliesh. *The Enchanted Book.*
Fenner. *Princesses & Peasant Boys.*
pb Grimm. *The Twelve Dancing Princesses.*
pb Lang. *The Twelve Dancing Princesses.*

PARALLEL: The Princess with the Golden Shoes (folktale)
Hatch. *More Danish Tales.*

PARALLEL: The Twelve Dancing Princesses (folktale)
Perrault. *Favorite Fairy Tales Told in France.*

Two of Everything (modern imaginative story)
Child Study Association of America. *Castles and Dragons.*
Ritchie. *The Treasure of Li-Po.*

The Ugly Duckling (modern imaginative story)
Andersen. *Andersen's Fairy Tales.*
Andersen. *Fairy Tales.*
Andersen. *It's Perfectly True.*
pb Andersen. *The Ugly Duckling.*
Rackham. *The Arthur Rackham Fairy Book.*

The Unlucky Shoes of Ali Abou (folktale)
Carpenter. *The Elephant's Bathtub.*

Urashima Taro and the Princess of the Sea (folktale)
Uchida. *The Dancing Kettle.*

Usha, the Mouse-Maiden (folktale)
pb Gobhai. *Usha, the Mouse-Maiden.*

When the Drum Sang (folktale)
pb Rockwell. *When the Drum Sang.*

PARALLEL: Little Sister and the Zimwi (folktale)
Aardema. *Tales for the Third Ear from Equatorial Africa.*

Who Was Tricked? (folktale)
pb Bowman. *Who Was Tricked?*

VARIANT: Pekka and the Rogues (folktale)
Bowman and Bianco. *Tales from a Finnish Tupa.*

Why the Bear Is Stumpy-tailed (folktale)
Arbuthnot. *Time for Fairy Tales.*
Asbjörnsen and Moe. *Favorite Fairy Tales Told in Norway.*
Hutchinson. *Fireside Stories.*
Jones. *Scandinavian Legends and Folk-Tales.*
Nixon. *Animal Legends.*
Undset. *True and Untrue.*

Why the Bear Sleeps All Winter (animal story)
Cathon and Schmidt. *Perhaps and Perchance.*

Why the Carabao's Hoof Is Split (folktale)
Sechrist. *Once in the First Times.*

Why the Dog and the Cat Are Not Friends (folktale)

ALSO CALLED: Why Dogs Hate Cats
Carpenter. *Tales of a Korean Grandmother.*
Lester. *The Knee-High Man.*

PARALLEL: The Magic Dumplings (folktale)
Sechrist and Woolsey. *It's Time for Story Hour.*

PARALLEL: Why Cats and Dogs Don't Like Each Other (folktale)
Buck. *The Chinese Story Teller.*

PARALLEL: Why the Cat and the Dog Cannot Live at Peace (folktale)
Deutsch and Yarmolinsky. *More Tales of Faraway Folk.*

Why the Sea Is Salt (folktale)
Asbjörnsen and Moe. *East of the Sun and West of the Moon.*
Asbjörnsen and Moe. *Favorite Fairy Tales Told in Norway.*
Gruenberg. *Favorite Stories Old and New.*
Lang. *Blue Fairy Book.*
Undset. *True and Untrue.*

PARALLEL: The Magic Mortar (folktale)
Uchida. *The Magic Listening Cap.*

PARALLEL: The Mill at the Bottom of the Sea (folktale)
Baker. *The Talking Tree.*

Why the Woodpecker Has a Long Nose (folktale)
Cathon and Schmidt. *Perhaps and Perchance.*

William Tell (Swiss legend)
Baldwin. *Favorite Tales of Long Ago.*
Buff. *The Apple and the Arrow.*
pb Hürlimann. *William Tell and His Son.*
Müller-Guggenbühl. *Swiss-Alpine Folk-Tales.*
Untermeyer. *The World's Great Stories.*

The Wise King and the Little Bee (Jewish legend)

ALSO CALLED: The Impudent Bee; The Wisdom of Solomon
Dobbs. *Once Upon a Time.*
Elkin. *The Wisest Man in the World.*
Freehof. *Stories of King Solomon.*
Gruenberg. *Favorite Stories Old and New.*

The Witch's Magic Cloth (modern imaginative story)
pb Matsutani. *The Witch's Magic Cloth.*

The Wonderful Knapsack (folktale)
Hatch. *13 Danish Tales.*

The Wonderful Pear Tree (folktale)
Carpenter. *Tales of a Chinese Grandmother.*

The Wonderful Pot (folktale)

ALSO CALLED: The Talking Pot
Association for Childhood Education International. *Told Under the
Green Umbrella.*
Hatch. *13 Danish Tales.*
Hutchinson. *Fireside Stories.*
Johnson, Sickels, and Sayers. *Anthology of Children's Literature.*

The Wonderful Tar-Baby (folktale)
Arbuthnot. *Time for Fairy Tales.*
Gruenberg. *Favorite Stories Old and New.*
Harris. *The Favorite Uncle Remus.*
Johnson, Sickels, and Sayers. *Anthology of Children's Literature.*

PARALLEL: The Dancing Palm Tree (folktale)
Walker. *The Dancing Palm Tree.*

PARALLEL: The Rabbit and the Clay Man (folktale)
Green. *Folktales and Fairy Tales of Africa.*

PARALLEL: Wakaima and the Clay Man (folktale)
Haviland. *The Fairy Tale Treasury.*

The Wonderful Wooden Peacock Flying Machine (folktale)
Tooze. *The Wonderful Wooden Peacock Flying Machine.*

Yanni (folktale)
Manning-Sanders. *A Book of Dragons.*

Stories of Special Interest
to Older Boys and Girls

And We Are as We Are (modern imaginative story)
　　Cathon and Schmidt. *Treasured Tales.*
　　Shannon. *Dobry,* pp. 24–26.

The Apple of Contentment (modern imaginative story)
　　Gruenberg. *Favorite Stories Old and New.*
　　Hazeltine. *Children's Stories to Read or Tell.*
　　Lines. *Tales of Magic and Enchantment.*
　　Pyle. *Pepper & Salt.*
　　Watson. *Tales for Telling.*

Baby Rainstorm (North American legend)
　　Fenner. *Time to Laugh.*
　　Rounds. *Ol' Paul, the Mighty Logger.*

Baldur (Norse myth)
　　ALSO CALLED: Balder and the Mistletoe; Baldur, the Beautiful; Baldur's
　　　　Doom; The Death of Balder; The Story of Balder
　　Arbuthnot. *Time for Fairy Tales.*
　　Baldwin. *The Story of Siegfried.*
　　Colum. *The Children of Odin.*
　　Hosford. *Thunder of the Gods.*
　　Johnson, Sickels, and Sayers. *Anthology of Children's Literature.*
　　Sellew. *Adventures with the Giants.*

The Ballad of the Harp Weaver (ballad story)
　　Arbuthnot. *Time for Poetry.*
　　Cole. *The Poet's Tales.*
　　Untermeyer. *Magic Circle.*

The Ballad of William Sycamore (ballad story)
Adshead. *An Inheritance of Poetry.*
Benét. *The Ballad of William Sycamore.*
Huffard. *My Poetry Book.*

Beowulf (Anglo-Saxon epic)

ALSO CALLED: Beowulf and the Fire Dragon; Grendel; Grendel the Monster;
The Song of Beowulf
Coolidge. *Legends of the North.*
Farjeon. *Mighty Men.*
Hosford. *By His Own Might.*
Schmitt. *The Heroic Deeds of Beowulf.*
Sutcliff. *Beowulf.*
Untermeyer. *The Firebringer.*

Bergamot (modern imaginative story)
Hoke. *Witches, Witches, Witches.*

Bertha Goldfoot (modern imaginative story)
Colwell. *A Second Storyteller's Choice.*
Farjeon. *The Old Nurse's Stocking-Basket.*

The Betrothal Feast (folktale)
Shannon. *Dobry,* pp. 133–38.

Betty Zane, Heroine of Fort Henry (modern realistic story)
Carmer. *A Cavalcade of Young Americans.*

The Blue Rose (folktale)
Frost. *Legends of the United Nations.*
Ross. *The Blue Rose.*
Shedlock. *The Art of the Story-Teller.*

A Bride for the Sea God (folktale)
Carpenter. *The Elephant's Bathtub.*

Chien-Nang (folktale)
Manning-Sanders. *A Book of Charms and Changelings.*

Childe Rowland (folktale)

ALSO CALLED: Childe Rowland and the King of Elfland
Finlay. *Folk Tales from the North.*
Manning-Sanders. *Stories from the English and Scottish Ballads.*
Williams-Ellis. *Fairy Tales from the British Isles.*

The Children of Lir (Celtic saga)

ALSO CALLED: The Swan Children
Colwell. *A Storyteller's Choice.*
Hodges. *The Other World.*
O'Faolain. *Irish Sagas and Folktales.*

Clever Manka (folktale)
Arbuthnot. *Time for Fairy Tales.*
Fillmore. *The Shepherd's Nosegay.*

PARALLEL: The Clever Peasant Girl (folktale)
Maas. *The Moon Painters.*

The Clever Prince (folktale)
Zinkin. *The Faithful Parrot.*

The Cow-Tail Switch (folktale)
Courlander and Herzog. *The Cow-Tail Switch.*

Daedalus and Icarus (Greek myth)

ALSO CALLED: Daedalus; The Flight of Icarus; Toward the Sun
Benson. *Stories of the Gods and Heroes.*
Coolidge. *Greek Myths.*
Gates. *Lord of the Sky: Zeus.*
Johnson, Sickels, and Sayers. *Anthology of Children's
Literature.*
Shippen. *A Bridle for Pegasus.*
Untermeyer. *The World's Great Stories.*

David and Goliath (Bible story)
Bible—Old Testament. I Samuel, chaps. 16–17.
Cathon and Schmidt. *Treasured Tales.*
De La Mare. *Stories from the Bible.*
De Regniers. *David and Goliath.*
Hodges. *Tell It Again.*
Petersham. *David.*
Untermeyer. *The Firebringer.*

Davy Crockett (North American legend)
Malcolmson. *Yankee Doodle's Cousins.*
Shapiro. *Yankee Thunder.*
Suddeth and Morenus. *Tales of the Western World.*

The Elephant's Child (modern imaginative story)
Arbuthnot. *Time for Fairy Tales.*
Gagliardo. *Let's Read Aloud.*
Gruenberg. *Favorite Stories Old and New.*
Huber. *Story and Verse for Children.*
Kipling. *The Elephant's Child.*
Kipling. *Just So Stories.* Illustrated by Etienne Delessert.
Kipling. *Just So Stories.* Illustrated by Nicholas.
Ross. *The Lost Half-Hour.*

Elsie Piddock Skips in Her Sleep (modern imaginative story)
Association for Childhood Education International. *Told Under the Magic Umbrella.*
Colwell. *A Storyteller's Choice.*

Feather o' My Wing (folktale)
Provensen. *The Provensen Book of Fairy Tales.*

PARALLEL: Three Feathers (folktale)
Jacobs. *More English Folk and Fairy Tales.*

The Fifty-First Dragon (modern imaginative story)
Broun. *The Fifty-First Dragon.*

Finn M'Cool and the Giant Cucullin (Celtic saga)

ALSO CALLED: The Bigger Giant; Fin M'Coul and Cucullin; Finn McCoul
Adams and Bacon. *A Book of Giant Stories.*
Green. *The Bigger Giant.*
Manning-Sanders. *A Book of Giants.*
Sleigh. *North of Nowhere.*

The Fisherman and the Genie (folktale)

ALSO CALLED: The Story of the Fisherman
Arabian Nights' Entertainments. *The Arabian Nights.* Edited by Padraic Colum.
Arabian Nights' Entertainments. *Arabian Nights.* Edited by Andrew Lang.
Arabian Nights' Entertainments. *The Arabian Nights: Their Best-Known Tales.* Edited by Wiggin and Smith.

The Fisherman and the Goblet (folktale)
Taylor. *The Fisherman and the Goblet.*

VARIANT: The Magic Crystal (folktale)
Graham. *The Beggar in the Blanket.*

Four Arrows (folktale)
Kelsey. *Once the Hodja.*

The Franklin's Tale (medieval legend)
Chaucer. *The Franklin's Tale.*

The Frog (folktale)
Ross. *The Buried Treasure.*
Sheehan. *A Treasury of Catholic Children's Stories.*

The Frog of Roland (modern imaginative story)
Cathon and Schmidt. *Treasured Tales.*

Gareth and Linette (medieval legend)

ALSO CALLED: How Gareth of Orkney Won His Spurs
Hodges. *The Other World.*
Lines. *Tales of Magic and Enchantment.*
Schiller. *The Kitchen Knight.*

Get Up and Bar the Door (ballad story)

ALSO CALLED: The Stubborn Sillies
Dobbs. *Once Upon a Time.*
Johnson, Sickels, and Sayers. *Anthology of Children's Literature.*
Rugoff. *A Harvest of World Folk Tales.*

The Giant Bones (folktale)
Alger. *Gaelic Ghosts.*

The Golden Fleece (Greek myth)

ALSO CALLED: The Argonauts; Jason; The Search for the Golden Fleece
Benson. *Stories of the Gods and Heroes.*
Colum. *The Golden Fleece.*
Gates. *The Warrior Goddess: Athena.*
Hawthorne. *A Wonder Book and Tanglewood Tales.*
Kingsley. *The Heroes.*
Untermeyer. *The Firebringer.*

The Golden Phoenix (folktale)
Barbeau. *The Golden Phoenix.*
Colwell. *A Second Storyteller's Choice.*

The Gypsy in the Ghost House (folktale)
Jagendorf and Tillhagen. *The Gypsies' Fiddle.*

The Happy Prince (modern imaginative story)
Harper. *Merry Christmas to You!*
Johnson. *The Harper Book of Princes.*
Wilde. *The Complete Fairy Tales of Oscar Wilde.*
Wilde. *The Happy Prince.*
Wilde. *The Selfish Giant.*

The Highwayman (ballad story)
Cook. *One Hundred and One Famous Poems.*
Ferris. *Favorite Poems Old and New.*
Noyes. *The Highwayman.*
Untermeyer. *The Golden Treasury of Poetry.*

Horatius at the Bridge (Roman legend)

ALSO CALLED: How Horatius Held the Bridge
Cook. *One Hundred and One Famous Poems.*
Fish. *The Boy's Book of Verse.*
Untermeyer. *The World's Great Stories* (prose).

How Thor's Hammer Was Lost and Found (Norse myth)

ALSO CALLED: The Hammer of Thor; How Thor Found His Hammer
Adams and Bacon. *A Book of Giant Stories.*
Arbuthnot. *Time for Fairy Tales.*
Coolidge. *Legends of the North.*
Power. *Bag O' Tales.*

Joan of Arc (modern realistic story)

ALSO CALLED: Jeanne d'Arc
Hazeltine. *Children's Stories to Read or Tell.*
Untermeyer. *The Firebringer.*

Joe Magarac (North American legend)

ALSO CALLED: Joe Magarac and His U.S.A. Citizen Papers;
    Steelmaker/Joe Magarac
Carmer. *America Sings.*
Jagendorf. *Upstate, Downstate.*
Leach. *The Rainbow Book of American Folk Tales and Legends.*
Malcolmson. *Yankee Doodle's Cousins.*
Shapiro. *Heroes in American Folklore.*
Shippen. *The Great Heritage.*
Stoutenburg. *American Tall Tales.*

John Henry (American legend)

ALSO CALLED: Steel Driving Man
Keats. *John Henry.*
Malcolmson. *Yankee Doodle's Cousins.*
Stein. *Steel Driving Man.*

Jorinda and Joringel (folktale)
Grimm. *Jorinda and Joringel.*
Grimm. *More Tales from Grimm.*
Lang. *Lilac Fairy Book.*

King Arthur and His Sword (medieval legend)

ALSO CALLED: King Arthur; The Marvel of the Sword; Of King Arthur;
The Sword in the Stone; The Winning of the Sword
Farjeon. *Mighty Men.*
Johnson, Sickels, and Sayers. *Anthology of Children's Literature.*
Malory. *The Boy's King Arthur.*
Pyle. *The Story of King Arthur and His Knights.*
Untermeyer. *The Firebringer.*
Watson. *Tales for Telling.*

The King of the Golden River (modern imaginative story)
Arbuthnot. *Time for Fairy Tales.*
Green. *Modern Fairy Stories.*
Ruskin. *The King of the Golden River.*

A Kiss from the Beautiful Fiorita (folktale)
Toor. *The Golden Carnation.*

The Knights of the Silver Shield (modern imaginative story)
Alden. *Why the Chimes Rang.*
Cathon and Schmidt. *Treasured Tales.*

The Lairdie with the Heart of Gold (folktale)
Alger. *Heather and Broom.*

The Laird's Lass and the Gobha's Son (folktale)
Alger. *Thistle and Thyme.*

The Last Lesson in French (modern imaginative story)

ALSO CALLED: The Last Lesson
Bryant. *How to Tell Stories to Children.*
Hodges. *Tell It Again.*

The Legend of Scarface (American Indian legend)

ALSO CALLED: Scarface
Davis. *A Baker's Dozen.*
Hazeltine. *Hero Tales from Many Lands.*
Watson. *Tales for Telling.*

The Legend of the Willow Plate (folktale)
Tresselt and Cleaver. *The Legend of the Willow Plate.*

The Little Dressmaker (modern imaginative story)
Farjeon. *The Little Bookroom.*
Tudor. *Tasha Tudor's Favorite Stories.*

The Loathly Lady (medieval legend)

ALSO CALLED: Sir Gawain and the Loathly Damsel
Troughton. *Sir Gawain and the Loathly Damsel.*
Westwood. *Medieval Tales.*

Loki . . . Apples of Youth (Norse myth)

ALSO CALLED: The Apples of Iduna; The Apples of Youth
Hosford. *Thunder of the Gods.*
Power. *Bag O' Tales.*
Untermeyer. *The Firebringer.*

Long, Broad, & Quickeye (folktale)

ALSO CALLED: The Broad Man, the Tall Man, and the Man with Eyes of
Flame; Long, Broad, and Sharpsight; Longshanks, Girth, and Keen
Fillmore. *The Shepherd's Nosegay.*
Lang. *Grey Fairy Book.*
Manning-Sanders. *A Book of Wizards.*
Ness. *Long, Broad, & Quickeye.*
Power. *Bag O' Tales.*

The Lost Half-Hour (modern imaginative story)
Provensen. *The Provensen Book of Fairy Tales.*
Ross. *The Lost Half-Hour.*

Love like Salt (folktale)
Leach. *The Soup Stone.*
Neufeld. *Beware the Man Without a Beard.*

The Magic Box (folktale)
Sawyer. *The Way of the Storyteller.*

The Maiden with the Black Wooden Bowl (folktale)

ALSO CALLED: The Maiden with the Wooden Helmet
Buck. *Fairy Tales of the Orient.*
Lang. *Violet Fairy Book.*
Sechrist and Woolsey. *It's Time for Story Hour.*

The Man o' the Clan (folktale)
Alger. *Gaelic Ghosts.*

The Man Who Didn't Believe in Ghosts (folktale)
Alger. *Ghosts Go Haunting.*

The Man Who Walked Widdershins round the Kirk (folktale)
Alger. *Ghosts Go Haunting.*

Mary, Mary, So Contrary! (folktale)
Fenner. *Fools and Funny Fellows.*
Fillmore. *The Shepherd's Nosegay.*

PARALLEL: The Pig-headed Wife (folktale)
Bowman and Bianco. *Tales from a Finnish Tupa.*

The Miraculous Pitcher (Greek myth)

ALSO CALLED: Baucis and Philemon
Hawthorne. *A Wonder Book and Tanglewood Tales.*
Hazeltine. *Children's Stories to Read or Tell.*
Sellew. *Adventures with the Gods.*
Untermeyer. *The Firebringer.*
Watson. *Tales for Telling.*

The Moor's Legacy (Spanish legend)
Irving. *The Alhambra.*
Smith. *Mystery Tales for Boys and Girls.*

Morgan and the Pot of Brains (folktale)
Pugh. *Tales from the Welsh Hills.*

PARALLEL: A Pottle o' Brains (folktale)
Jacobs. *More English Folk and Fairy Tales.*

The Mousewife (modern imaginative story)
Colwell. *A Storyteller's Choice.*
Godden. *The Mousewife.*

The Nightingale (modern imaginative story)
Andersen. *Andersen's Fairy Tales.*
Andersen. *Fairy Tales.*
Andersen. *It's Perfectly True.*
Andersen. *The Nightingale.* Illustrated by Harold Berson.
Andersen. *The Nightingale.* Illustrated by Nancy Ekholm Burkert.
Andersen. *The Nightingale and the Emperor.*
Johnson, Sickels, and Sayers. *Anthology of Children's Literature.*
Lang. *Yellow Fairy Book.*
Shedlock. *The Art of the Story-Teller.*

The Painted Eyebrow (folktale)
Carpenter. *Tales of a Chinese Grandmother.*

Paul Bunyan (North American legend)

ALSO CALLED: The Sky Bright Axe/Paul Bunyan
Felton. *Legends of Paul Bunyan.*
McCormick. *Paul Bunyan Swings His Axe.*
Stevens. *Paul Bunyan.*
Stoutenburg. *American Tall Tales.*

Pegasus (Greek myth)

ALSO CALLED: Bellerophon; The Chimaera
Carpenter. *Wonder Tales of Horses and Heroes.*
Hawthorne. *A Wonder Book and Tanglewood Tales.*
Johnson, Sickels, and Sayers. *Anthology of Children's Literature.*
Price. *Myths and Enchantment Tales.*
Turska. *Pegasus.*
Untermeyer. *The Firebringer.*

Perseus (Greek myth)

ALSO CALLED: The Gorgon's Head; How Perseus Slew the Gorgon;
The Story of Perseus
Benson. *Stories of the Gods and Heroes.*
Colum. *The Golden Fleece.*
Gates. *The Warrior Goddess: Athena.*
Hawthorne. *A Wonder Book and Tanglewood Tales.*
Hodges. *The Gorgon's Head.*
Johnson, Sickels, and Sayers. *Anthology of Children's Literature.*
Kingsley. *The Heroes.*
Raymond. *Famous Myths of the Golden Age.*
Untermeyer. *The Firebringer.*

Phaeton (Greek myth)

ALSO CALLED: How Phaeton Drove the Horses of the Sun
Benson. *Stories of the Gods and Heroes.*
Bulfinch. *A Book of Myths.*
Johnson, Sickels, and Sayers. *Anthology of Children's Literature.*
Raymond. *Famous Myths of the Golden Age.*
Untermeyer. *The Firebringer.*

The Prince and the Goose Girl (modern imaginative story)
Johnson. *The Harper Book of Princes.*
Provensen. *The Provensen Book of Fairy Tales.*

The Princess and the Vagabone (folktale)
Johnson. *The Princesses.*
Ross. *The Blue Rose.*
Sawyer. *The Way of the Storyteller.*

PARALLEL: Graylegs (folktale)
Hatch. *More Danish Tales.*

PARALLEL: King Thrushbeard (folktale)
Grimm. *King Thrushbeard.* Illustrated by Felix Hoffmann.
Grimm. *King Thrushbeard.* Illustrated by Kurt Werth.

Princess of the Full Moon (folktale)
Guirma. *Princess of the Full Moon.*

The Princess of Tomboso (folktale)
Barbeau. *The Golden Phoenix.*

PARALLEL: The Nose (folktale)
Grimm. *Fairy Tales.* Illustrated by Jean O'Neill.

PARALLEL: Too Much Nose (folktale)
Zemach. *Too Much Nose.*

The Princess with One Accomplishment (modern imaginative story)
Cathon and Schmidt. *Treasured Tales.*

A Proper Lesson for Those Who Would Burden Asses with Learning (folktale)
Eulenspiegel. *Tyll Ulenspiegel's Merry Pranks.*

VARIANT: Donkey and Scholars (folktale)
Jagendorf. *Noodlehead Stories.*

The Reluctant Dragon (modern imaginative story)
Grahame. *The Reluctant Dragon.*
Green. *Modern Fairy Stories.*

Ride on the Wind (modern realistic story)

ALSO CALLED: A Matter of Mathematics
Dalgliesh. *Ride on the Wind.*
Shippen. *A Bridle for Pegasus.*

Rikki-Tikki-Tavi (modern imaginative story)
Kipling. *The Jungle Book.*

Rip Van Winkle (North American legend)
Field. *American Folk and Fairy Tales.*
Irving. *Rip Van Winkle.*
Rackham. *The Arthur Rackham Fairy Book.*

PARALLEL: Keel-Wee, a Korean Rip Van Winkle (folktale)
Jewett. *Which Was Witch?*

Roland and Oliver (French epic)

ALSO CALLED: A Roland for an Oliver
Baldwin. *The Story of Roland.*
Hazeltine. *Hero Tales from Many Lands.*
Picard. *French Legends, Tales, and Fairy Stories.*
Untermeyer. *The World's Great Stories.*

Sandy MacNeil and His Dog (folktale)
Alger. *Gaelic Ghosts.*

The Shooting Match at Nottingham Town (ballad story)

ALSO CALLED: Robin Hood and the Golden Arrow
Malcolmson. *Song of Robin Hood.*
Pyle. *The Merry Adventures of Robin Hood.*
Pyle. *Some Merry Adventures of Robin Hood.*

Shrewd Todie & Lyzer the Miser (folktale)
Singer. *When Shlemiel Went to Warsaw.*

The Skillful Huntsman (modern imaginative story)
Arbuthnot. *Time for Fairy Tales.*
Pyle. *Pepper & Salt.*

Sohrab and Rustem (Persian epic)

ALSO CALLED: Rustem and Sohrab
Brockett. *Persian Fairy Tales.*
Picard. *Tales of Ancient Persia.*
Untermeyer. *The Firebringer.*

The Soul of the Great Bell (Chinese legend)

ALSO CALLED: The Voice of the Great Bell
Hodges. *Tell It Again.*
Sechrist. *Thirteen Ghostly Yarns.*

The Stone Lion (folktale)

ALSO CALLED: The Story of the Stone Lion
Davis. *A Baker's Dozen.*
Manning-Sanders. *A Book of Magical Beasts.*

The Swineherd (modern imaginative story)
Andersen. *Andersen's Fairy Tales.*
Andersen. *It's Perfectly True.*
Andersen. *The Swineherd.*
Dalgliesh. *The Enchanted Book.*
Johnson, Sickels, and Sayers. *Anthology of Children's Literature.*
Sechrist and Woolsey. *It's Time for Story Hour.*

VARIANT: How the Princess's Pride Was Broken (modern imaginative story)
Pyle. *The Wonder Clock.*

The Tale of the Earl of Mar's Daughter (folktale)
Alger. *By Loch and by Lin.*

Talk (folktale)
Courlander and Herzog. *The Cow-Tail Switch.*
Gruenberg. *Favorite Stories Old and New.*

The Tell-Tale Heart (modern imaginative story)
Poe. *The Pit and the Pendulum.*
Poe. *Tales and Poems.*

The Terrible Stranger (Celtic epic)

ALSO CALLED: The Champion of Ireland
Fenner. *Adventure: Rare and Magical.*
Hodges. *The Other World.*

VARIANT: Sir Gawain and the Green Knight (medieval legend)
Hieatt. *Sir Gawain and the Green Knight.*
Serraillier. *The Challenge of the Green Knight.*

Theseus (Greek myth)

ALSO CALLED: The Minotaur
Colum. *The Golden Fleece.*
Hawthorne. *A Wonder Book and Tanglewood Tales.*
Kingsley. *The Heroes.*
Mayne. *William Mayne's Book of Heroes.*
Untermeyer. *The World's Great Stories.*

Thor . . . How The Thunderer Was Tricked (Norse myth)

ALSO CALLED: A Contest with the Giants; Thor and Loki in the Giants' City;
Thor and the Giant King; Thor's Unlucky Journey
Colum. *The Children of Odin.*
Coolidge. *Legends of the North.*
Hosford. *Thunder of the Gods.*
Sellew. *Adventures with the Giants.*
Untermeyer. *The Firebringer.*

The Thousandth Gift (modern imaginative story)
Picard. *The Mermaid and the Simpleton.*

The Three Men of Power—Evening, Midnight, and Sunrise (folktale)
Ransome. *Old Peter's Russian Tales.*

To Your Good Health! (folktale)
Fenner. *Princesses & Peasant Boys.*
Haviland. *Favorite Fairy Tales Told in Russia.*
Lang. *Crimson Fairy Book.*
Shedlock. *The Art of the Story-Teller.*

The Tsarina's Greatest Treasure (folktale)
Spicer. *Long Ago in Serbia.*

A Week of Sundays (modern imaginative story)
Gruenberg. *Favorite Stories Old and New.*

What Ailed the King (modern imaginative story)
Cathon and Schmidt. *Treasured Tales.*

The White Horse Girl and the Blue Wind Boy (modern imaginative story)
Davis. *A Baker's Dozen.*
Sandburg. *Rootabaga Stories.*
Sechrist and Woolsey. *It's Time for Story Hour.*

Why the Sea Moans (folktale)
Cathon and Schmidt. *Perhaps and Perchance.*
Sheehan. *Folk and Fairy Tales from Around the World.*

Why Women Talk More than Men (American Indian myth)
Fisher. *Stories California Indians Told.*

The Wise Witness (folktale)
Borski. *Good Sense and Good Fortune.*

PARALLEL: The Eggs (folktale)
Brandenberg. *The Eggs.*

Woman's Wit (modern imaginative story)
Fenner. *Demons and Dervishes.*
Pyle. *Twilight Land.*

The Wooden Horse (Greek epic)

ALSO CALLED: The Trojan Horse; The Trojan War
Benson. *Stories of the Gods and Heroes.*
Reeves. *The Trojan Horse.*
Untermeyer. *The World's Great Stories.*

The Yellow Ribbon (folktale)
Leach. *The Rainbow Book of American Folk Tales and Legends.*
Sheehan. *Folk and Fairy Tales from Around the World.*

You Never Can Tell (folktale)
Holland. *You Never Can Tell.*

Stories for
Holiday Programs

CHRISTMAS

Babouscka (Russian legend)

ALSO CALLED: Baboushka and the Three Kings; The Legend of Babouscka
pb Robbins. *Baboushka and the Three Kings.*
Smith and Hazeltine. *The Christmas Book of Legends & Stories.*
The Tall Book of Christmas.
Wernecke. *Christmas Stories from Many Lands.*

The Birth of Jesus (Bible story)

Bible—New Testament. Luke, chap. 2, vs. 8–20; Matthew, chap. 2, vs. 1–11.
pb Bible—New Testament. *The Christ Child.*

y **Brownies—It's Christmas!** (modern imaginative story)
pb Adshead. *Brownies—It's Christmas!*

The Christmas Apple (modern imaginative story)

ALSO CALLED: The Little Clock-Maker
Bishop. *Happy Christmas!*
Harper. *Merry Christmas to You!*
Ross. *The Lost Half-Hour.*
Sawyer. *This Way to Christmas,* pp. 51–60.

Christmas at Greccio (medieval legend)

ALSO CALLED: St. Francis and the First Christmas Crèche
Jewett. *God's Troubadour.*
Sechrist and Woolsey. *It's Time for Christmas.*
Smith and Hazeltine. *The Christmas Book of Legends & Stories.*

The Christmas Cuckoo (modern imaginative story)
Browne. *Granny's Wonderful Chair.*
Harper. *Merry Christmas to You!*
Olcott. *Good Stories for Great Holidays.*

y **Christmas Eve in the Used Car Lot** (modern imaginative story)
Child Study Association of America. *Holiday Storybook.*

The Christmas Promise (modern imaginative story)
Sawyer. *This Way to Christmas,* pp. 92–104.

The Christmas Spider (folktale)
Eaton. *The Animals' Christmas.*

The Christmas That Was Nearly Lost (modern imaginative story)
Sawyer. *This Way to Christmas,* pp. 133–45.

y **The Christmas Visitors** (folktale)
pb Winter. *The Christmas Visitors.*

y **The Christmas Window** (modern imaginative story)
pb Manifold. *The Christmas Window.*

Cosette's Christmas (modern realistic story)
Bishop. *Happy Christmas!*

The Dwarf and the Cobbler's Sons (folktale)
Harper. *Merry Christmas to You!*

VARIANT: Schnitzle, Schnotzle, and Schnootzle (folktale)
Sawyer. *The Long Christmas.*

y **The Elves and the Shoemaker** (folktale)

ALSO CALLED: The Shoemaker and the Elves
Arbuthnot. *Time for Fairy Tales.*
Association for Childhood Education International. *Told Under the Green Umbrella.*
pb Grimm. *The Elves and the Shoemaker.*
Grimm. *Favorite Fairy Tales Told in Germany.*
Grimm. *More Tales from Grimm.*
pb Grimm. *The Shoemaker and the Elves.*

MODERN VERSION: Brownies—Hush! (modern imaginative story)
pb Adshead. *Brownies—Hush!*

y **The Fir Tree** (modern imaginative story)
Andersen. *Andersen's Fairy Tales.*
Andersen. *Fairy Tales.*
Andersen. *The Fir Tree.*
Andersen. *It's Perfectly True.*

Giant Grummer's Christmas (modern imaginative story)
The Tall Book of Christmas.

y **The Gift** (modern imaginative story)
pb Balet. *The Gift.*

y **The Golden Cobwebs** (modern imaginative story)
Bryant. *How to Tell Stories to Children.*

y **How Mrs. Santa Claus Saved Christmas** (modern imaginative story)
McGinley. *How Mrs. Santa Claus Saved Christmas* (verse).

How the Good Gifts Were Used by Two (modern imaginative story)
Fenner. *Fools and Funny Fellows.*
Pyle. *The Wonder Clock.*
Watson. *Tales for Telling.*

In Clean Hay (modern realistic story)
Association for Childhood Education International. *Told Under the Christmas Tree.*
Harper. *Merry Christmas to You!*

In the Great Walled Country (modern imaginative story)
Alden. *Why the Chimes Rang.*
Association for Childhood Education International. *Told Under the Christmas Tree.*

The Juggler of Notre Dame (French legend)

ALSO CALLED:The Little Juggler; Our Lady's Juggler
Cooney. *The Little Juggler.*
Sawyer. *The Way of the Storyteller.*
Todd. *The Juggler of Notre Dame.*
Untermeyer. *The Firebringer.*

VARIANT: The Clown of God (French legend)
Smith and Hazeltine. *The Christmas Book of Legends & Stories.*

The Legend of St. Christopher (saint legend)
Olcott. *Good Stories for Great Holidays.*
Shedlock. *The Art of the Story-Teller.*
Smith and Hazeltine. *The Christmas Book of Legends & Stories.*

The Legend of the Christmas Rose (German legend)
Bruderhof Communities. *Behold That Star.*
Harper. *Merry Christmas to You!*
Smith and Hazeltine. *The Christmas Book of Legends & Stories.*

The Little Blind Shepherd (modern realistic story)
Sechrist and Woolsey. *It's Time for Christmas.*

y **The Little Engine That Could** (modern imaginative story)
pb Piper. *The Little Engine That Could.*

y **The Little Green Elf's Christmas** (modern imaginative story)
Bailey and Lewis. *Favorite Stories for the Children's Hour.*

The Little Pagan Faun (modern imaginative story)
Association for Childhood Education International. *Told Under the Christmas Tree.*
Colwell. *A Storyteller's Choice.*
Eaton. *The Animals' Christmas.*
Green. *Tales of Make-Believe.*

y **Little Piccola** (modern imaginative story)
Olcott. *Good Stories for Great Holidays.*

y **The Littlest Angel** (modern imaginative story)
pb Tazewell. *The Littlest Angel.*

y **Lullaby** (Polish legend)
Association for Childhood Education International. *Told Under the Christmas Tree.*

y **The Night Before Christmas** (modern imaginative story)
ALSO CALLED: A Visit from St. Nicholas
Bishop. *Happy Christmas!* (verse).
pb Moore. *The Night Before Christmas* (verse).

y **Noël for Jeanne-Marie** (modern imaginative story)
pb Seignobosc. *Noël for Jeanne-Marie.*

The Nutcracker (modern imaginative story)
Chappell. *The Nutcracker.*
Walden. *The Nutcracker.*

y **One Thousand Christmas Beards** (modern imaginative story)
pb Duvoisin. *One Thousand Christmas Beards* (verse).

y **Paddy's Christmas** (modern imaginative story)
pb Monsell. *Paddy's Christmas.*

The Poor Count's Christmas (modern imaginative story)
Harper. *Merry Christmas to You!*

y **The Puppy Who Wanted a Boy** (modern imaginative story)
Child Study Association of America. *Holiday Storybook.*

Silent Night, the Story of a Song (modern realistic story)
Pauli. *Silent Night, the Story of a Song.*

The Silver Hen (modern imaginative story)
Ross. *The Lost Half-Hour.*

Sing for Christmas (music)
Wheeler. *Sing for Christmas* (for each of twenty-four Christmas carols—
the score and the story of how the carol came to be).

A Star for Hansi (modern realistic story)
Association for Childhood Education International. *Told Under the
Christmas Tree.*
Vance. *A Star for Hansi.*
Wernecke. *Christmas Stories from Many Lands.*

The Story of Brother Johannick and His Silver Bell (French legend)
Colwell. *A Second Storyteller's Choice.*

y **The Tailor of Gloucester** (modern imaginative story)
pb Potter. *The Tailor of Gloucester.*

The Third Lamb (modern imaginative story)
Smith and Hazeltine. *The Christmas Book of Legends & Stories.*

This Is the Christmas (folktale)
The Horn Book Magazine, 20, no. 6 (Nov.–Dec. 1944), 501–09.
Sawyer. *Joy to the World.*
Sawyer. *This Is the Christmas.*

Torten's Christmas Secret (modern imaginative story)
Dolbier. *Torten's Christmas Secret.*

The Trapper's Tale of the First Birthday (modern imaginative story)
ALSO CALLED:Gifts for the First Birthday.
Fenner. *Feasts and Frolics.*
Sawyer. *This Way to Christmas*, pp. 116–22.
Sechrist and Woolsey. *It's Time for Christmas.*

y **'Twas in the Moon of Wintertime** (American Indian legend)
pb Abisch. *'Twas in the Moon of Wintertime.*

The Voyage of the Wee Red Cap (modern imaginative story)
Association for Childhood Education International. *Told Under the Christmas Tree.*
Sawyer. *The Long Christmas.*
Sawyer. *This Way to Christmas*, pp. 32–44.

The Wee Christmas Cabin of Carn-na-ween (modern imaginative story)
Sawyer. *The Long Christmas.*
Wernecke. *Christmas Stories from Many Lands.*

Where Love Is, There God Is Also (modern realistic story)
ALSO CALLED: Where Love Is, God Is
Bishop. *Happy Christmas!*
Colwell. *A Storyteller's Choice.*
Smith and Hazeltine. *The Christmas Book of Legends & Stories.*

Why the Chimes Rang (modern imaginative story)
Alden. *Why the Chimes Rang.*
pb Alden. *Why the Chimes Rang.*

The Wishing Well (folktale)
Sawyer. *The Long Christmas.*

The Wooden Shoes of Little Wolff (modern imaginative story)
ALSO CALLED: The Sabot of Little Wolff
Harper. *Merry Christmas to You!*
Olcott. *Good Stories for Great Holidays.*

The Worker in Sandalwood (modern imaginative story)
The Atlantic Monthly, 104 (December 1909), 786.
Bruderhof Communities. *Behold That Star.*
Sechrist and Woolsey. *It's Time for Christmas.*

EASTER

The Apple Tree (modern imaginative story)
Harper. *Easter Chimes.*

y **Bidushka Lays an Easter Egg** (modern realistic story)
Child Study Association of America. *Holiday Storybook.*
Jones. *Maminka's Children.*

The Boy Who Discovered the Spring (modern imaginative story)
Alden. *Why the Chimes Rang and Other Stories.*

y **The Country Bunny and the Little Gold Shoes** (modern imaginative story)
pb Heyward. *The Country Bunny and the Little Gold Shoes.*

y **The Easter Bunny That Overslept** (modern imaginative story)
pb Friedrich. *The Easter Bunny That Overslept.*

y **The Egg Tree** (modern realistic story)
pb Milhous. *The Egg Tree.*

y **The Golden Egg Book** (modern imaginative story)
pb Brown. *The Golden Egg Book.*

y **Juanita** (modern realistic story)
pb Politi. *Juanita.*

A Lesson of Faith (modern imaginative story)
Hazeltine and Smith. *The Easter Book of Legends and Stories.*
Olcott. *Good Stories for Great Holidays.*

y **Miss Suzy's Easter Surprise** (modern imaginative story)
pb Young. *Miss Suzy's Easter Surprise.*

Persephone and Demeter (Greek myth)

ALSO CALLED: Demeter and Persephone; Persephone and the Springtime;
    The Pomegranate Seeds; Proserpina and the Pomegranate Seeds
Aulaire, d'. *D'Aulaires' Book of Greek Myths.*
Colum. *The Golden Fleece.*
Frost. *Legends of the United Nations.*
Hawthorne. *A Wonder Book and Tanglewood Tales.*
pb Hodges. *Persephone and the Springtime.*
Sellew. *Adventures with the Gods.*

y **The Remarkable Egg** (modern imaginative story)
pb Holl. *The Remarkable Egg.*

The Resurrection (Bible story)
Bible—New Testament. John, chap. 20.

The Selfish Giant (modern imaginative story)
Colwell. *A Storyteller's Choice.*
Green. *Modern Fairy Stories.*
Harper. *Easter Chimes.*
Sheehan. *A Treasury of Catholic Children's Stories.*
pb Wilde. *The Selfish Giant.*

Stealing the Springtime (American Indian myth)
Cothran. *With a Wig, with a Wag.*
Field. *American Folk and Fairy Tales.*
Schauffler. *The Days We Celebrate,* vol. 2.

y **The Sugar Egg** (modern imaginative story)
Harper. *Easter Chimes.*

The Velveteen Rabbit (modern imaginative story)
Bianco. *The Velveteen Rabbit.*

y **The Whiskers of Ho Ho** (modern imaginative story)
pb Littlefield. *The Whiskers of Ho Ho.*

y **The World in the Candy Egg** (modern imaginative story)
pb Tresselt. *The World in the Candy Egg.*

HALLOWEEN

The Bold Dragoon (North American legend)
ALSO CALLED: The Adventure of My Grandfather
Irving. *The Bold Dragoon.*
Sechrist. *Heigh-Ho for Halloween!*
Sechrist. *Thirteen Ghostly Yarns.*

The Buried Moon (folktale)
pb Jacobs. *The Buried Moon.*
Jacobs. *More English Folk and Fairy Tales.*

The Conjure Wives (folktale)
Harper. *Ghosts and Goblins.*
Sechrist. *Heigh-Ho for Halloween!*
Sechrist and Woolsey. *It's Time for Story Hour.*

y **The Craziest Hallowe'en** (modern imaginative story)
pb Von Hippel. *The Craziest Hallowe'en.*

y **Elisabeth the Cow Ghost** (modern imaginative story)
pb Du Bois. *Elisabeth the Cow Ghost.*
Gruenberg. *Favorite Stories Old and New.*

y **The Fierce Yellow Pumpkin** (modern imaginative story)
Gruenberg. *Favorite Stories Old and New.*

y **Georgie to the Rescue** (modern imaginative story)
pb Bright. *Georgie to the Rescue.*

The Ghost Dog of South Mountain (folktale)
Carpenter. *Wonder Tales of Dogs and Cats.*

y **The Goblin Under the Stairs** (modern imaginative story)
pb Calhoun. *The Goblin Under the Stairs.*

The Hobyahs (folktale)
Fenner. *Giants & Witches and a Dragon or Two.*
Jacobs. *More English Folk and Fairy Tales.*

y **Horace the Happy Ghost** (modern imaginative story)
Child Study Association of America. *Holiday Storybook.*

The Hungry Old Witch (folktale)
Davis. *A Baker's Dozen.*
Fenner. *Giants & Witches and a Dragon or Two.*
Finger. *Tales from Silver Lands.*
Harper. *Ghosts and Goblins.*
Hoke. *Witches, Witches, Witches.*

y **The Jack-o'-Lantern** (modern realistic story)
Association for Childhood Education International. *Told Under the Blue Umbrella.*

The Jack-o'-Lantern Witch (modern realistic story)
Pannell and Cavanah. *Holiday Round Up.*

Katcha and the Devil (folktale)
Fillmore. *The Shepherd's Nosegay.*
Ross. *The Blue Rose.*

The King o' the Cats (folktale)
Harper. *Ghosts and Goblins.*
Jacobs. *More English Folk and Fairy Tales.*
pb Jacobs. *The Pied Piper.*
Johnson, Sickels, and Sayers. *Anthology of Children's Literature.*
Olcott. *Good Stories for Great Holidays.*
Williams-Ellis. *Fairy Tales from the British Isles.*

The Legend of Sleepy Hollow (North American legend)
Irving. *Rip Van Winkle and the Legend of Sleepy Hollow.*

The Long Leather Bag (folktale)
Wiggin and Smith. *The Fairy Ring.*

PARALLEL: Old Gally Mander (folktale)
Field. *American Folk and Fairy Tales.*
Hoke. *Witches, Witches, Witches.*

PARALLEL: The Old Witch (folktale)
Harper. *Ghosts and Goblins.*
Jacobs. *More English Folk and Fairy Tales.*

The Magic Ball (folktale)
Fenner. *Feasts and Frolics.*
Finger. *Tales from Silver Lands.*
Hoke. *Witches, Witches, Witches.*

The Mountain Witch and the Peddler (folktale)
Uchida. *The Magic Listening Cap.*

My Grandfather Hendry Watty (modern imaginative story)
Sechrist. *Thirteen Ghostly Yarns.*
Smith. *Mystery Tales for Boys and Girls.*

y **One Dark Night** (modern imaginative story)
pb Preston. *One Dark Night.*

Peter and the Witch of the Wood (folktale)
Hoke. *Witches, Witches, Witches.*

The Phantom Knight of the Vandal Camp (medieval legend)
Olcott. *Good Stories for Great Holidays.*

The Roll-Call of the Reef (modern realistic story)
Fenner. *Ghosts, Ghosts, Ghosts.*
Smith. *Mystery Tales for Boys and Girls.*
Van Thal. *Famous Tales of the Fantastic.*

Schippeitaro (folktale)
Sechrist and Woolsey. *It's Time for Story Hour.*
Sheehan. *Folk and Fairy Tales from Around the World.*
Wiggin and Smith. *The Fairy Ring.*

y **Space Witch** (modern imaginative story)
pb Freeman. *Space Witch.*

y **The Strange Visitor** (folktale)
De La Mare. *Animal Stories* (verse).
Jacobs. *English Folk and Fairy Tales.*
Molin. *Ghosts, Spooks, & Spectres.*
Olcott. *Good Stories for Great Holidays.*
Sechrist. *Heigh-Ho for Halloween!*
Williams-Ellis. *Fairy Tales from the British Isles.*

Tamlane (ballad story)
Harper. *Ghosts and Goblins.*
Jacobs. *More English Folk and Fairy Tales.*
Johnson, Sickels, and Sayers. *Anthology of Children's Literature.*
Watson. *Tales for Telling.*
Williams-Ellis. *Fairy Tales from the British Isles.*

PARALLEL: Tam Lin (folktale)
Hodges. *The Other World.*
Wilson. *Scottish Folk-Tales and Legends.*

y **Teeny-Tiny** (folktale)
Harper. *Ghosts and Goblins.*
Hutchinson. *Fireside Stories.*
Jacobs. *English Folk and Fairy Tales.*
Sechrist. *Heigh-Ho for Halloween!*
Watson. *Tales for Telling.*

y **Tilly Witch** (modern imaginative story)
pb Freeman. *Tilly Witch.*

The Tinker and the Ghost (folktale)
Boggs and Davis. *Three Golden Oranges.*
Fenner. *Feasts and Frolics.*
Johnson, Sickels, and Sayers. *Anthology of Children's Literature.*

Which Was Witch? (folktale)
Arbuthnot. *Time for Fairy Tales.*
Hoke. *Witches, Witches, Witches.*
Jewett. *Which Was Witch?*

The Witches' Ride (folktale)
Harper. *Ghosts and Goblins.*

y **Wobble the Witch Cat** (modern imaginative story)
pb Calhoun. *Wobble the Witch Cat.*

y **A Woggle of Witches** (modern imaginative story)
pb Adams. *A Woggle of Witches.*

The Woodman and the Goblins (modern imaginative story)
Harper. *Ghosts and Goblins.*

Zini and the Witches (American Indian legend)
Colwell. *A Second Storyteller's Choice.*

JEWISH HOLIDAYS

At the Seder (Passover)
Gamoran. *Hillel's Happy Holidays.*

The Cruse of Oil—165 B.C. (Hanukkah)
Association for Childhood Education International. *Told Under the Christmas Tree.*

Esther . . . Who Saved Her People (Purim)
Untermeyer. *The Firebringer.*

Grandmother's Tale (Hanukkah)
Singer. *Zlateh the Goat.*

A Great Miracle (Hanukkah)
Morrow. *A Great Miracle.*

The Magician (Passover)
pb Shulevitz. *The Magician.*

Start with Something Sweet (Rosh Hashana)
Child Study Association of America. *Holiday Storybook.*

Succos
　　Taylor. *All-of-a-Kind Family,* pp. 166–75.

Yom Kippur, Day of Atonement
　　Taylor. *More All-of-a-Kind Family,* pp. 25–38.

MOTHER'S DAY

Cornelia's Jewels (Roman legend)
　　ALSO CALLED: Cornelia
　　Baldwin. *Favorite Tales of Long Ago.*
　　Olcott. *Good Stories for Great Holidays.*
　　Untermeyer. *The World's Great Stories.*

Mama and the Graduation Present (modern realistic story)
　　Forbes. *Mama's Bank Account,* pp. 120–27.
　　Pannell and Cavanah. *Holiday Round Up.*

y **Mr. Rabbit and the Lovely Present** (modern imaginative story)
　　pb Zolotow. *Mr. Rabbit and the Lovely Present.*

y **My Mother and I** (modern realistic story)
　　pb Fisher. *My Mother and I.*

My Mother Is the Most Beautiful Woman in the World (folktale)
　　Hodges. *Tell It Again.*
　　Pannell and Cavanah. *Holiday Round Up.*
　　Reyher. *My Mother Is the Most Beautiful Woman in the World.*

NEW YEAR'S DAY

The Forest Full of Friends (modern imaginative story)
　　Alden. *Why the Chimes Rang and Other Stories.*

The Little Match Girl (modern imaginative story)
　　Andersen. *Andersen's Fairy Tales.*
　　Andersen. *Fairy Tales.*
　　Andersen. *It's Perfectly True.*
　　pb Andersen. *The Little Match Girl.*

y **Mei Li** (modern realistic story)
　　pb Handforth. *Mei Li.*

Ring in the New! (modern realistic story)
Pannell and Cavanah. *Holiday Round Up.*

The Twelve Months (folktale)
Dalgliesh. *The Enchanted Book.*
Haviland. *Favorite Fairy Tales Told in Czechoslovakia.*
Johnson, Sickels, and Sayers. *Anthology of Children's Literature.*
Olcott. *Good Stories for Great Holidays.*
Wiggin and Smith. *The Fairy Ring.*

PATRIOTIC DAYS

y **Abraham Lincoln** (modern realistic story: Lincoln's Birthday)
pb Aulaire, d'. *Abraham Lincoln.*
Foster. *Abraham Lincoln.*

Better Than a Parade (modern realistic story: Memorial Day)
Child Study Association of America. *Holiday Storybook.*

Columbus (modern realistic story: Columbus Day)
pb Aulaire, d'. *Columbus.*
Dalgliesh. *The Columbus Story.*
Graham. *Christopher Columbus, Discoverer.*

Columbus and the Egg (modern realistic story: Columbus Day)
Olcott. *Good Stories for Great Holidays.*
Untermeyer. *The World's Great Stories.*

MODERN VERSION: Journey on Eggs (modern imaginative story)
Lawson. *I Discover Columbus,* pp. 23–30.

The Flagmakers (modern imaginative story: Flag Day)
Cathon and Schmidt. *Treasured Tales.*

y **George Washington** (modern realistic story: Washington's Birthday)
pb Aulaire, d'. *George Washington.*
Foster. *George Washington.*

George Washington and His Hatchet (North American legend: Washington's Birthday)
ALSO CALLED: I Cannot Tell a Lie
Baldwin. *Favorite Tales of Long Ago.*
Botkin. *A Treasury of American Folklore.*

Grace Bedell and Lincoln's Beard, Why the President Wore Whiskers
   (modern realistic story: Lincoln's Birthday)
   Carmer. *A Cavalcade of Young Americans.*

The Peterkins Celebrate the "Fourth" (modern realistic story: Fourth of July)
   Fenner. *Feasts and Frolics.*
   Hale. *The Peterkin Papers.*

Star-Spangled Banner Girl (modern realistic story: Flag Day)
   Bailey. *Children of the Handcrafts.*

ST. PATRICK'S DAY

y **The Hungry Leprechaun** (modern imaginative story)
pb Calhoun. *The Hungry Leprechaun.*

Murdoch's Rath (modern imaginative story)
   Sechrist and Woolsey. *It's Time for Story Hour.*

The Old Hag of the Forest (folktale)
   Hoke. *Witches, Witches, Witches.*

y **Patrick O'Donnell and the Leprechaun** (folktale)
   Haviland. *Favorite Fairy Tales Told in Ireland*

The Peddler of Ballaghadereen (folktale)
   Fenner. *Feasts and Frolics.*
   Sawyer. *The Way of the Storyteller.*

Saint Patrick and the Last Snake (saint legend)
   Child Study Association of America. *Holiday Storybook.*
   Pannell and Cavanah. *Holiday Round Up.*

ST. VALENTINE'S DAY

y **Appolonia's Valentine** (modern realistic story)
pb Milhous. *Appolonia's Valentine.*

Cupid and Psyche (Greek myth)
   Arbuthnot. *Time for Fairy Tales.*
   Coolidge. *Greek Myths.*
   Johnson, Sickels, and Sayers. *Anthology of Children's Literature.*

Olcott. *Good Stories for Great Holidays.*
Price. *Myths and Enchantment Tales.*
Untermeyer. *The Firebringer.*

Juan Brings a Valentine (modern realistic story)
Child Study Association of America. *Holiday Storybook.*

The Valentine Box (modern realistic story)
Lovelace. *The Valentine Box.*
Pannell and Cavanah. *Holiday Round Up.*

THANKSGIVING

y **Cranberry Thanksgiving** (modern realistic story)
pb Devlin. *Cranberry Thanksgiving.*

The First Thanksgiving (modern realistic story)
Barksdale. *The First Thanksgiving.*
Child Study Association of America. *Holiday Storybook.*
Dalgliesh. *The Thanksgiving Story.*

The Huckabuck Family (modern imaginative story)
Harper. *The Harvest Feast.*
Sandburg. *Rootabaga Stories.*

Indians for Thanksgiving (modern realistic story)
Harper. *The Harvest Feast.*
Sechrist and Woolsey. *It's Time for Thanksgiving.*

The Kingdom of the Greedy (modern imaginative story)
Harper. *The Harvest Feast.*
Watson. *Tales for Telling.*

y **Little Bear's Thanksgiving** (modern imaginative story)
pb Brustlein. *Little Bear's Thanksgiving.*

y **Old Man Rabbit's Thanksgiving Dinner** (modern imaginative story)
Harper. *The Harvest Feast.*

y **The Plymouth Thanksgiving** (modern realistic story)
pb Weisgard. *The Plymouth Thanksgiving.*

The Pudding That Broke Up a Preaching (folktale)
Credle. *Tall Tales from the High Hills.*
Luckhardt. *Thanksgiving: Feast and Festival.*

The Pumpkin Giant (modern imaginative story)
Davis. *A Baker's Dozen.*
Harper. *The Harvest Feast.*
Ross. *The Lost Half-Hour.*
Sechrist. *Heigh-Ho for Halloween!*
Watson. *Tales for Telling.*
pb Wilkins. *The Pumpkin Giant.*

y **A Quick-running Squash** (modern imaginative story)
Harper. *The Harvest Feast.*

Thankful (modern realistic story)
Fenner. *Feasts and Frolics.*

Aids for the Storyteller

Armstrong, Helen. "Hero Tales for Telling." *The Horn Book Magazine,* 16 (May 1940), 7–15.

Bryant, S. C. *How to Tell Stories to Children.* Houghton, 1924. Reprint. Gale, 1971.

Burrell, Arthur. *A Guide to Storytelling.* Pitman, 1926. Reprint. Gale, 1971.

Children's Services Division—Storytelling Materials Survey Committee. *For Storytellers and Storytelling: Bibliographies, Materials, and Resource Aids.* American Library Association, 1968.

Colum, Padraic. *Storytelling New and Old.* Macmillan, 1968.

Colwell, Eileen, ed. *A Storyteller's Choice: A Selection of Stories, with Notes on How to Tell Them.* Walck, 1964.

Cooke, Elizabeth. *The Ordinary and the Fabulous: An Introduction to Myths, Legends, and Fairy Tales for Teachers and Storytellers.* Cambridge, 1971.

Fitzgerald, B. S. *World Tales for Creative Dramatics and Storytelling.* Prentice, 1962.

Greene, Ellin, ed. *Stories: A List of Stories to Tell and Read Aloud.* 6th ed. New York Public Library, 1968.

Greene, Ellin, and Schoenfeld, Madalynne, eds. *A Multimedia Approach to Children's Literature: A Selective List of Films, Filmstrips, and Recordings Based on Children's Books.* American Library Association, 1972.

Hardendorff, Jeanne, ed. *Stories to Tell.* 5th ed. Enoch Pratt Free Library, 1965.

Horn Book Magazine, The. Storytelling Number, 10 (May 1934).

Johnson, Edna; Sickels, E. R.; and Sayers, F. C., eds. *Anthology of Children's Literature.* 4th rev. ed. Houghton, 1970, pp. 1141–47.

Lyman, Edna. *Story Telling: What to Tell and How to Tell It.* 3rd ed. Gale, 1971.

Moore, Vardine. *Pre-School Story Hour.* 2d ed. Scarecrow, 1972.

Nesbitt, Elizabeth. "The Art of Storytelling." *The Horn Book Magazine,* 21 (November 1945), 439–44.

Nesbitt, Elizabeth. "Hold to That Which Is Good." *The Horn Book Magazine*, 16 (May 1940), 7–15.

Okun, Lilian. *Let's Listen to a Story*. Wilson, 1959 (pamphlet). Introduction, pp. 9–16 (radio storytelling).

Peterson, E. F. "The Pre-School Hour." *Top of the News*, 18, no. 2 (December 1961), 47–51.

Recordings for Children: A Selected List of Records and Cassettes. 3rd ed. New York Library Association, Children's and Young Adult Services Section, 1972.

Ross, E. S., ed. *The Lost Half-Hour: A Collection of Stories*. Harcourt, 1963, pp. 181–91.

Sawyer, Ruth. *How to Tell a Story*. Compton, 1965 (pamphlet).

Sawyer, Ruth. *The Way of the Storyteller*. Viking, 1942.

Shedlock, M. L. *The Art of the Storyteller*. Foreword by Anne Carroll Moore. Rev. ed. Dover, 1951.

Spain, F. L., ed. "A Storyteller's Approach to Children's Books." *The Contents of the Basket*. New York Public Library, 1960, pp. 51–59.

Storytelling. Illinois Libraries Children's Issue, 51, no. 1 (January 1969).

Classified List of Stories

ACTION STORIES

I'm Going on a Bear Hunt, 8
Tale of a Black Cat, The, 13

Twist-Mouth Family, The, 15

AFRO-AMERICANS

John Henry, 57
Magic Lollipop, The, 9
Pumpkinseeds, 12
Sam, 12
Snowy Day, The, 13

Steel Driving Man, 57
Sunflowers for Tina, 13
Valentine Box, The, 82
Whistle for Willie, 16

AMERICAN INDIANS. *See* LEGENDS—American Indian;
MYTHS—American Indian; STORIES BY COUNTRY—
United States of America (regional): American Indian

ANIMAL STORIES

Adventurous Mouse, The, 3
Androcles and the Lion, 17
Angus and the Ducks, 3
Animal Musicians, The, 4
Animals' Peace Day, The, 3
Armadillo Who Had No Shell, The, 3
Ask Mr. Bear, 3

Away Went Wolfgang!, 3
Bear's Toothache, The, 4
Beautiful Blue Jay, The, 18
Bedtime for Frances, 4
Bell of Atri, The, 18
Belling the Cat, 9
Billy Goat in the Chili Patch, The, 4

Blind Men and the Elephant, The, 19
Blueberries for Sal, 4
Bremen Town Musicians, The, 4
Caps for Sale, 10
Cat and the Parrot, The, 20
Cat at Night, The, 5
Circus Baby, The, 5
Clever Turtle, The, 22
Cock, the Mouse, and the
  Little Red Hen, The, 5
Country Bunny and the
  Little Gold Shoes, The, 73
Crocodile's Tale, A, 5
Curious George Takes a Job, 5
Dance of the Animals, 23
Dancing Cow, The, 23
Dandelion, 5
Dick Whittington and His Cat, 23
Drakesbill and His Friends, 5
Easter Bunny That Overslept, The, 73
Elephant and the Bad Baby, The, 6
Elephant's Child, The, 54
Escape of the Animals, The, 25
Extraordinary Tug-of-War, The, 45
Frederick, 6
From Tiger to Anansi, 27
Giant and the Rabbit, The, 27
Golden Apple, The, 7
Golden Egg Book, The, 73
Good Night, Owl!, 7
Grateful Beasts, The, 29
Guinea Pig's Tale, The, 7
Gunniwolf, The, 7
Half-Chick, The, 7
Happy Lion, The, 7
Hare and the Hedgehog, The, 30
Harry the Dirty Dog, 7
Henny-Penny, 7
How Spider Got a Thin Waist, 30
How the Camel Got His Hump, 30
How the Camel Got His
  Proud Look, 30
How the Dog Became the
  Servant of Man, 30

How the Hare Told the Truth About
  His Horse, 30
How the Manx Cat Lost Its Tail, 30
How the Porcupine Outwitted
  the Fox, 31
How the Robin's Breast
  Became Red, 31
How the Siamese Cats Got the
  Kink in the End of Their Tails, 31
Hungry Spider and the Turtle, 31
In the Forest, 8
Jackal and the Alligator, The, 32
Jenny's Birthday Book, 8
Kindai and the Ape, 17
King o' the Cats, The, 76
King of the Birds, The, 8
King's Choice, The, 8
Kuratko the Terrible, 21
Lion and the Mouse, The, 8
Little Bear, 8
Little Hatchy Hen, 8
Little White Hen, The, 9
Lullaby, 70
Make Way for Ducklings, 9
Meeting of the Young Mice, The, 9
Mighty Mikko, 39
Millions of Cats, 10
Miss Suzy's Easter Surprise, 73
Mr. Brown and Mr. Gray, 10
Mr. Gumpy's Outing, 10
Mr. Rabbit and Mr. Bear, 36
Monkeys and the Little Red
  Hats, The, 10
Mousewife, The, 59
Nanabozho and the Wild Geese, 37
Neighbors, The, 10
Old Acquaintance Is Soon Forgot!, 37
Old Man Rabbit's Thanksgiving
  Dinner, 82
Once a Mouse, 11
One Fine Day, 11
One Silver Second, 12
One Who Wasn't Afraid, The, 37
Otto and the Magic Potatoes, 38

Outside Cat, The, 12
Owl and the Woodpecker, The, 12
Paddy's Christmas, 71
Partnership of Rabbit and Elephant,
and What Came of It, The, 38
Peter and the Twelve-Headed
Dragon, 24
Peter and the Wolf, 38
Play with Me, 12
Priceless Cats, The, 23
Puss in Boots, 39
Rosie's Walk, 12
Runaway Bunny, The, 12
Sacred Amulet, The, 41
Story About Ping, The, 13
Story of Chicken-Licken, The, 7
Story of Ferdinand, The, 13
Story of Pancho and the Bull with
the Crooked Tail, The, 13
Surprise Party, The, 13
Tailor of Gloucester, The, 71
Tale of Johnny Town-Mouse, The, 15
Tale of Peter Rabbit, The, 13
Talking Cat, The, 43
Three Bears, The, 14
Three Billy Goats Gruff, The, 14
Three Little Animals, 14
Three Little Pigs, The, 14
Three Little Pigs and the Ogre, The, 44

Timid Timothy, 15
Tomten, The, 15
Too Much Noise, 11
Torten's Christmas Secret, 72
Tortoise Talked, The, 46
Tug of War, A, 45
Turtle Who Couldn't Stop
Talking, The, 46
Ugly Duckling, The, 46
Ungrateful Tiger, The, 44
Whiskers of Ho Ho, The, 74
Who Took the Farmer's Hat?, 16
Why Cats Always Wash After Eating, 16
Why Cats and Dogs Don't Like
Each Other, 47
Why Cats Wash After Meals, 16
Why Dogs Hate Cats, 47
Why the Bear Is Stumpy-tailed, 47
Why the Bear Sleeps All Winter, 47
Why the Carabao's Hoof Is Split, 47
Why the Dog and the Cat Are
Not Friends, 47
Why the Jackal Won't Speak to
the Hedgehog, 16
Why the Woodpecker Has a
Long Nose, 48
Wolf and the Seven Kids, The, 16
Wonderful Tar-Baby, The, 48

BALLAD STORIES

Ballad of the Harp Weaver, The, 51
Ballad of William Sycamore, The, 52
Get Up and Bar the Door, 55
Highwayman, The, 56
I Know an Old Lady, 32
King John and the Abbot of
Canterbury, 33

Little Old Lady Who Swallowed a
Fly, The, 32
Robin Hood and the Golden Arrow, 62
Shooting Match at Nottingham
Town, The, 62
Tamlane, 77

BIBLE STORIES

Birth of Jesus, The, 67
Daniel in the Lion's Den, 23
David and Goliath, 53
Esther . . . Who Saved Her
   People, 78
Joseph and His Brothers, 33

Moses Delivers the People of
   Israel, 37
Moses in the Bulrushes,10
Noah and the Ark, 11
Resurrection, The, 74

BLINDNESS

Little Blind Shepherd, The, 70

This Is the Christmas, 71

CUMULATIVE AND REPETITIVE STORIES

All in the Morning Early, 3
Bun, The, 6
Don't Count Your Chicks, 10
Egg of Fortune, The, 9
Elephant and the Bad Baby, The, 6
Giacco and His Bean, 15
Gingerbread Boy, The, 6
Gingerbread Man, The, 6
Great Big Enormous Turnip, The, 15
Henny-Penny, 7
House That Jack Built, The, 8
I Know an Old Lady, 32
Johnny-Cake, 6
Journey Cake, Ho!, 6
Lad and the Fox, The, 10
Little Old Lady Who Swallowed a
   Fly, The, 32
Little White Hen, The, 9
Milkmaid and Her Pail, The, 9

Millions of Cats, 10
Nanny Who Wouldn't Go
   Home to Supper, 11
Old Woman and Her Pig, The, 11
One Dark Night, 76
Pancake, The, 6
Rooster and the Hen, The, 11
Runaway Sardine, The, 6
Story of Chicken-Licken, The, 7
Talk, 63
Teeny-Tiny, 77
Three Bears, The, 14
Three Billy Goats Gruff, The, 14
Three Little Pigs, The, 14
Tikki Tikki Tembo, 45
Travels of a Fox, The, 15
Turnip, The, 15
Who Took the Farmer's Hat?, 16
Why the Sun Was Late, 16

DRAGONS

Dragon and His Grandmother, The, 24
Dragonmaster, 24
Fifty-First Dragon, The, 54
Peter and the Twelve-Headed
   Dragon, 24

Reluctant Dragon, The, 62
Tears of the Dragon, The, 43
Wonderful Dragon of Timlin, The, 16
Yanni, 49

ECOLOGY

Lorax, The, 35   Smoke, 13

EPICS AND SAGAS

Anglo-Saxon   *French*
Beowulf, 52   Roland and Oliver, 62

Celtic   *Greek*
Champion of Ireland, The, 63   Trojan Horse, The, 65
Children of Lir, The, 53   Wooden Horse, The, 65
Finn M'Cool and the Giant
  Cucullin, 54   *Persian*
Terrible Stranger, The, 63   Sohrab and Rustem, 63

ETHICAL AND SOCIAL VALUES

And We Are as We Are, 51   Kindai and the Ape, 17
Animals' Peace Day, The, 3   King of the Golden River, The, 57
Apple of Contentment, The, 51   King Solomon's Carpet, 33
Betty Zane, Heroine of Fort Henry, 52 King's Choice, The, 8
Boy Who Cried Wolf, The, 4   Knights of the Silver Shield,
Boy Without a Name, The, 19   The, 57
Budulinek, 20   Last Lesson in French, The, 57
Bundle of Sticks, A, 4   Legend of St. Christopher, The, 70
Can Men Be Such Fools as All   Magic Box, The, 58
  That?, 20   Magic Feather Duster, The, 9
Christmas Apple, The, 67   Mama and the Graduation Present, 79
Christmas Cuckoo, The, 68   Mr. Brown and Mr. Gray, 10
Dutch Boy and the Dike, The, 24   One Silver Second, 12
Edie Changes Her Mind, 5   Pied Piper of Hamelin, The, 38
Eggs, The, 65   Plain Princess, The, 38
Elephant and the Bad Baby, The, 6   Prince Bertram the Bad, 12
Frog of Roland, The, 55   Princess of the Full Moon, 61
George Washington and His   Princess with One
  Hatchet, 80   Accomplishment, The, 61
Golden Touch, The, 28   Rolling Rice Ball, The, 40
Horatius at the Bridge, 56   Swineherd, The, 63
How the Princess's Pride Was   Thankful, 83
  Broken, 63   Three Gold Pieces, 43
How the Robin's Breast Became   Toads and Diamonds, 45
  Red, 31   Wave, The, 20

What Ailed the King, 64
Why Cats and Dogs Don't Like
Each Other, 47

Wise Man on the Mountain, The, 11
You Never Can Tell, 65

FABLES

Androcles and the Lion, 17
Belling the Cat, 9
Blind Men and the Elephant, The, 19
Boy Who Cried Wolf, The, 4
Bundle of Sticks, A, 4
Foolish, Timid Rabbit, The, 7
Fox and the Crow, The, 21
Girl Monkey and the String of
Pearls, The, 28
How to Weigh an Elephant, 25

Lion and the Mouse, The, 8
Milkmaid and Her Pail, The, 9
Monkey and the Crocodile, The, 37
Once a Mouse, 11
Stolen Necklace, The, 13, 28
Talkative Tortoise, The, 46
Town Mouse and the Country
Mouse, The, 15
Turtle Who Couldn't Stop
Talking, The, 46

FLIGHT

Daedalus and Icarus, 53
Flying Ship, The, 26
King Solomon's Carpet, 33
Pegasus, 60

Perseus, 60
Phaeton, 61
Ride on the Wind, 62

FOLKTALES BY COUNTRY

*Africa**
Clever Turtle, The, 22
How Spider Got a Thin Waist, 30
Hungry Spider and the Turtle, 31
Kindai and the Ape, 17
Little Sister and the Zimwi, 47
Nomi and the Magic Fish, 22
Partnership of Rabbit and Elephant,
and What Came of It, The, 38
Rabbit and the Clay Man, The, 49
Story, a Story, A, 43
Tug of War, A, 45

Wakaima and the Clay Man, 49
When the Drum Sang, 46
Why the Sun Was Late, 16
See also FOLKTALES—Congo,
Ethiopia, Ghana, Liberia,
Rhodesia, South Africa, Tunisia,
Upper Volta

Arabia
Aladdin; or, The Wonderful Lamp, 17
Ali Baba and the Forty Thieves, 26
Anklet of Jewels, The, 21
Fisherman and the Genie, The, 54
Forty Thieves, The, 26

*See p. x for an explanation of this
classification.

Armenia
King and the Shepherd, The, 33
Miller-King, The, 40
One Fine Day, 11
Shrovetide, 30

Austria
Schnitzle, Schnotzle, and
  Schnootzle, 68

Bohemia
Dragonmaster, 24
Long, Broad, & Quickeye, 58
Long, Broad, and Sharpsight, 58

Borneo
Lazy Tok, 35

Brazil
Golden Gourd, The, 28
Parrot of Limo Verde, The, 38
Tug of War, The, 45
Why the Sea Moans, 65

Bulgaria
Betrothal Feast, The, 52
Escape of the Animals, The, 25
Gift from the Heart, A, 28
Grandmother Marta, 29

Burma
Grateful Beasts, The, 29
Master Kho and the Tiger, 44

Canada
Golden Phoenix, The, 55
Princess of Tomboso, The, 61

MICMAC INDIAN
Little Scarred One, The, 22

Ceylon
Bride for the Sea God, A, 52
Invisible Silk Robe, The, 25

Wonderful Wooden Peacock Flying
  Machine, The, 49

China
Blue Rose, The, 52
Chien-Nang, 52
8,000 Stones, 24
Five Queer Brothers, The, 6
Girl Who Could Think, The, 28
How the Camel Got His Proud
  Look, 30
Legend of the Willow Plate, The, 58
Ma Lien and the Magic Brush, 35
Magic Dumplings, The, 47
Orange Tree King, The, 40
Painted Eyebrow, The, 60
Three Gifts, The, 34
Tikki Tikki Tembo, 45
Tortoise Talked, The, 46
Why Cats and Dogs Don't Like
  Each Other, 47
Wonderful Pear Tree, The, 48
You Never Can Tell, 65

Congo
Magic Tree, The, 36

Costa Rica
Witches' Ride, The, 78

Czechoslovakia
Broad Man, the Tall Man, and the
  Man with Eyes of Flame, The, 58
Budulinek, 20
Clever Manka, 53
Katcha and the Devil, 76
Kuratko the Terrible, 21
Longshanks, Girth, and Keen, 58
Three Golden Hairs, The, 44
Twelve Months, The, 80

Denmark
Buried Treasure, The, 20
Doctor and Detective Too, 23

Fat Cat, The, 21
Graylegs, 61
Mill at the Bottom of the Sea, The, 48
Per and the North Wind, 34
Peter Ox, 38
Princess with the Golden
    Shoes, The, 46
Wonderful Knapsack, The, 48
Wonderful Pot, The, 48

Ecuador
Search for the Magic Lake, The, 41

Egypt
False Friend, The, 25

England
Buried Moon, The, 74
Cap o' Rushes, 22
Cat and the Parrot, The, 20
Catskin, 22
Chanticleer and the Fox, The, 21
Childe Rowland, 52
Childe Rowland and the King of
    Elfland, 52
Cock, the Mouse, and the Little
    Red Hen, The, 5
Dick Whittington and His Cat, 23
Fifty Red Night-Caps, 10
Gingerbread Boy, The, 6
Gingerbread Man, The, 6
Hare and the Hedgehog, The, 30
Henny-Penny, 7
Hereafterthis, 30
Hobyahs, The, 75
House That Jack Built, The, 8
Jack and the Beanstalk, 32
Johnny-Cake, 6
King o' the Cats, The, 76
Lazy Jack, 34
Master of All Masters, 36
Mr. Vinegar, 10
Molly Whuppie, 36
Old Witch, The, 76

Old Woman and Her Pig, The, 11
Old Woman Who Lived in a
    Vinegar Bottle, The, 25
Pied Piper of Franchville, The, 38
Pottle o' Brains, A, 59
Slip! Slop! Gobble!, 21
Sneezy Snatcher and Sammy Small, 42
Strange Visitor, The, 77
Teeny-Tiny, 77
Three Bears, The, 14
Three Feathers, 54
Three Little Pigs, The, 14
Three Sillies, The, 44
Three Wishes, The, 14
Tom Thumb, 45
Tom Tit Tot, 40

Estonia
Clever Peasant Girl, The, 53

Ethiopia
Adventurous Mouse, The, 3
Farmer and the King, The, 25
Goat Well, The, 28
Husband Who Wanted to Mind
    the House, The, 31
Mammo the Fool, 36
Meeting of the Young Mice, The, 9
Storyteller, The, 43

Finland
End of the World, The, 7
Forest Bride, The, 26
Mary, Mary, So Contrary!, 59
Mighty Mikko, 39
Pekka and the Rogues, 47
Pig-headed Wife, The, 59
Rooster and the Hen, The, 11
Ship That Sailed by Land and
    Sea, The, 26
Who Was Tricked?, 47

Flanders
Donkey and Scholars, 61
Why Cats Wash After Meals, 16

France
Beauty and the Beast, 18
Cinderella, 21
Drakesbill and His Friends, 5
Mouse-Princess, The, 26
Puss in Boots, 39
Sleeping Beauty, The, 41
Stone Soup, 43
Three Oranges, The, 44
Toads and Diamonds, 45
Twelve Dancing Princesses, The, 46
Wishing Well, The, 72

Germany
Ashputtel, 21
Brave Little Tailor, The, 20
Bremen Town Musicians, The, 4
Doctor Know-It-All, 23
Dragon and His Grandmother, The, 24
Dwarf and the Cobbler's Sons, The, 68
Earth Gnome, The, 24
Elves and the Shoemaker, The, 68
Fisherman and His Wife, The, 25
Frog Prince, The, 27
Golden Goose, The, 28
Hans in Luck, 29
Hansel and Gretel, 29
Jorinda and Joringel, 57
King Thrushbeard, 61
No Room, 11
Nose, The, 61
One-Eye, Two-Eyes, and
    Three-Eyes, 37
Proper Lesson for Those Who Would
    Burden Asses with Learning, A, 61
Prudent Hans, 34
Rapunzel, 40
Rumpelstiltskin, 40
Snow White and the Seven Dwarfs, 42
Sorcerer's Apprentice, The, 42
Thorn Rose, 42
Three Golden Hairs of the King of
    the Cave Giants, The, 44
Twelve Dancing Princesses, The, 46

Wishing Table, the Gold Donkey, and
    the Cudgel-in-the-Sack, The, 34
Wolf and the Seven Kids, The, 16

Ghana
Talk, 63

Greece
Eggs, The, 65
Love like Salt, 58
Three Gold Pieces, 43

Guatemala
Sacred Amulet, The, 41

Honduras
How the Porcupine Outwitted
    the Fox, 31

Hungary
Gypsy Fiddle, The, 29
Lamb with the Golden Fleece, The, 28
Little Cockerel, The, 35
Little Rooster and the Turkish
    Sultan, The, 35
Seven Simons, The, 26
Silver Penny, The, 41
Sultan's Bath, The, 13

India
Beautiful Blue Jay, The, 18
Blind Man and the Deaf Man, The, 19
Blind Man, the Deaf Man, and the
    Donkey, The, 19
Cat and the Parrot, The, 20
Clever Prince, The, 53
Ghost Who Was Afraid of Being
    Bagged, The, 27
Horse-Egg, The, 23
How the Dog Became the Servant of
    Man, 30
Jackal and the Alligator, The, 32
King's Choice, The, 8
Legend of the Orange
    Princess, The, 35

Magic Bottles, The, 35
Moon Princess, The, 37
Princess of the Mountain, The, 39
Stolen Necklace, The, 13, 28
Tiger, the Brahman, and the
Jackal, The, 44
Usha, the Mouse-Maiden, 46

Indonesia
Princess of the Rice Fields, The, 39

Iran
Joco and the Fishbone, 32
Mirza and the Ghul, 36

Iraq
Unlucky Shoes of Ali Abou, The, 46

Ireland
Bigger Giant, The, 54
Billy Beg and the Bull, 18
Clever Wife, The, 22
Crochera, The, 27
Donal O'Ciaran from Connaught, 20
Feather o' My Wing, 54
Hudden and Dudden and Donald
O'Neary, 31
Jack and His Comrades, 4
Jack and the Friendly Animals, 4
Long Leather Bag, The, 76
Molly and the Giant, 36
Mop Servant, The, 37
Old Hag of the Forest, The, 81
Patrick O'Donnell and the
Leprechaun, 81
Peddler of Ballaghadereen, The, 81
Princess and the Vagabone, The, 61
Two Bottles, The, 36
Well o' the World's End, The, 27
White Hen, The, 41

Isle of Man
How the Manx Cat Lost Its Tail, 30

Israel
Chanina and the Angels, 21
Seven-Year Blessing, The, 41

Italy
Aniello, 17
Cenerentola, 22
Cobbler, The, 20
Crumb in His Beard, A, 23
Donkey Which Made Gold, The, 34
Giacco and His Bean, 15
King Clothes, 29
Kiss from the Beautiful Fiorita, A, 57
Magic Box, The, 58
Priceless Cats, The, 23
Rags-and-Tatters, 40
Too Much Nose, 61
Wonderful Stone, The, 18
Zezolla and the Date-Palm Tree, 22

Jamaica
Quarrel, The, 40

Japan
Boy Who Drew Cats, The, 19
Burning of the Rice Fields, The, 20
Child in the Bamboo Grove, The, 21
Funny Little Woman, The, 27
Issun Boshi, the Inchling, 45
Magic Mortar, The, 47
Maiden with the Black Wooden
Bowl, The, 59
Maiden with the Wooden
Helmet, The, 59
Mountain Witch and the
Peddler, The, 76
Old Woman and Her Dumpling, The, 27
One for the Price of Two, 37
Princess of Light, The, 21
Schippeitaro, 77
Tengu's Magic Nose Fan, 43
Terrible Leak, The, 43

Urashima Taro and the Princess of
the Sea, 46
Wave, The, 20

Korea
Keel-Wee, a Korean Rip Van
Winkle, 62
Three Wishes, The, 14
Which Was Witch?, 78
Why the Dog and the Cat Are Not
Friends, 47

Latvia
Princess on the Glass
Mountain, The, 39

Liberia
Cow-Tail Switch, The, 53

Lithuania
I Am Your Misfortune, 31

Macedonia
Yanni, 49

Majorca
Gardener, the Abbot, and the
King, The, 33
Tony Di-Moany, 34

Mexico
Billy Goat in the Chili Patch, The, 4
Giant and the Rabbit, The, 27

Morocco
Boy Without a Name, The, 19

The Netherlands
King's Rijstepap, The, 33
Why Cats Always Wash After
Eating, 16

Nigeria
Dancing Palm Tree, The, 49
Extraordinary Tug-of-War, The, 45
Why the Sun and Moon Live in
the Sky, 16

Norway
Boots and His Brothers, 19
Cat and the Parrot, The, 20
Christmas Visitors, The, 68
East of the Sun and West of
the Moon, 24
Giant Who Had No Heart in His
Body, The, 27
Gudbrand on the Hillside, 29
Happy-Go-Lucky, 29
Husband Who Was to Mind the
House, The, 31
Jesper Who Herded the Hares, 41
Kari Woodengown, 22
Lad Who Went to the North
Wind, The, 33
Nanny Who Wouldn't Go Home
to Supper, 11
Pancake, The, 6
Parson and the Clerk, The, 33
Princess on the Glass Hill, The, 39
Princess Whom No One Could
Silence, The, 39
Squire's Bride, The, 42
Three Billy Goats Gruff, The, 14
Why the Bear Is Stumpy-tailed, 47
Why the Sea Is Salt, 47

Philippine Islands
Crocodile's Tale, A, 5
Why the Carabao's Hoof Is Split, 47

Poland
As the World Pays, 44
Christmas Spider, The, 68
Golden Lynx, The, 28
Jolly Tailor Who Became King, The, 32

Look, There Is a Turtle Flying, 46
Magical Crock, The, 35
Wise Witness, The, 65

Portugal
Monkey's Pomegranate, The, 11
Pedro de Malas Artes, or, Clumsy
    Pedro, 34

Puerto Rico
Animal Musicians, The, 4
Dance of the Animals, 23
Oté, 38

Rhodesia
How a Poor Man Was Rewarded, 30

Romania
Prince Loaf, 39
Why the Woodpecker Has a
    Long Nose, 48

Russia
Baba Yaga and the Little Girl with
    the Kind Heart, 18
Beetle, 18
Blabbermouth, 19
Bun, The, 6
Flying Ship, The, 26
Giant and the Dwarf, The, 27
Golden Fish, The, 25
Great Big Enormous Turnip, The, 15
How the Peasant Kept House, 31
It Could Be Worse, 11
Kojata, 33
Mitten, The, 10
Mixed-up Feet and the Silly
    Bridegroom, The, 34
Monastery of No Cares, The, 37
My Mother Is the Most Beautiful
    Woman in the World, 79
Neighbors, The, 10
Old Acquaintance Is Soon Forgot!, 37

One Who Wasn't Afraid, The, 37
Pancakes and Pies, 35
Peter and the Wolf, 38
Salt, 41
Seven Simeons, The, 26
Shrewd Todie & Lyzer the Miser, 62
Silly Goose War, The, 19
Snegourka, the Snow Maiden, 42
Snow Maiden, The, 42
Snowflake, 42
Tamara and the Sea Witch, 43
Three Men of Power—Evening,
    Midnight, and Sunrise, The, 64
To Your Good Health!, 64
Turnip, The, 15
Vasilisa the Beautiful, 22
Why the Cat and the Dog Cannot
    Live at Peace, 47

Scotland
All in the Morning Early, 3
Giant Bones, The, 55
Lairdie with the Heart of Gold, The, 57
Laird's Lass and the Gobha's
    Son, The, 57
Man o' the Clan, The, 59
Man Who Didn't Believe in Ghosts,
    The, 59
Man Who Walked Widdershins round
    the Kirk, The, 59
Sandy MacNeil and His Dog, 62
Tale of the Earl of Mar's
    Daughter, The, 63
Tam Lin, 77
Whippety Stourie, 41

Serbia
Egg of Fortune, The, 9
This Is the Christmas, 71
Tsarina's Greatest Treasure, The, 64

South Africa
When the Husband Stayed Home, 31

Spain
Black Magic, 19
Flea, The, 26
Frog, The, 55
Half-Chick, The, 7
Sack of Truth, The, 41
Three Golden Oranges, 44
Tinker and the Ghost, The, 77

Sudan
Monkeys and the Little Red
  Hats, The, 10

Sweden
Lad and the Fox, The, 10
Nail Soup, 43
Old Woman and the Tramp, The, 43
Peter and the Witch of the Wood, 76
Three Wishes, The, 14

Switzerland
Red-Chicken, 5
Silly Jean, 34
Three Sneezes, The, 43

Thailand
How the Siamese Cats Got the Kink
  in the End of Their Tails, 31

Tibet
Stone Lion, The, 63

Tunisia
Why the Jackal Won't Speak to
  the Hedgehog, 16

Turkey
Baldpate, 18
Donkey Egg, The, 23
Four Arrows, 55
Guest for Halil, A, 29
How Many Donkeys?, 30
Ifrit and the Magic Gifts, The, 32

Keloğlan and the Ooh-Genie, 34
Nazar the Brave, 20
Sixty at a Blow, 20

United States of America
Catskins, 22
Conjure Wives, The, 75
Cow in the House, A, 11
Ghost Dog of South Mountain, The, 75
Jack and the Bean Tree, 32
Jack and the North West Wind, 34
Jack and the Robbers, 4
Jack and the Varmints, 20
Legs of the Moon, The, 35
Mr. Rabbit and Mr. Bear, 36
Ogre, the Sun, and the Raven, The, 37
Old Gally Mander, 76
Old One-Eye, 37
Presentneed, Bymeby, and
  Hereafter, 30
Pudding That Broke Up a
  Preaching, The, 83
Soap, Soap, Soap!, 42
Sody Sallyraytus, 14
Travels of a Fox, The, 15
Whitebear Whittington, 24
Why Dogs Hate Cats, 47
Wonderful Tar-Baby, The, 48
Yellow Ribbon, The, 65

Upper Volta
Princess of the Full Moon, 61

Uruguay
Hungry Old Witch, The, 75

Venezuela
Magic Ball, The, 76

Vietnam
Chu Cuoi's Trip to the Moon, 21
Fisherman and the Goblet, The, 54

Jeweled Slipper, The, 22
Magic Crystal, The, 54
Ungrateful Tiger, The, 44

Wales
Morgan and the Pot of Brains, 59

West Indies
From Tiger to Anansi, 27
Madam Crab Loses Her Head, 35
Tiger Story, Anansi Story, 27

Yugoslavia
Laughing Prince, The, 34

GHOSTS

Elisabeth the Cow Ghost, 75
Georgie to the Rescue, 75
Ghost Dog of South Mountain, The, 75
Ghost Who Was Afraid of Being
  Bagged, The, 27
Giant Bones, The, 55
Horace the Happy Ghost, 75
Jimmy Takes Vanishing Lessons, 32

Man o' the Clan, The, 59
Man Who Didn't Believe in
  Ghosts, The, 59
Man Who Walked Widdershins
  round the Kirk, The, 59
Sandy MacNeil and His Dog, 62
Tinker and the Ghost, The, 77

GIANTS

Bigger Giant, The, 54
Billy Beg and the Bull, 18
Crochera, The, 27
Finn M'Cool and the Giant
  Cucullin, 54
Giant and the Dwarf, The, 27
Giant and the Rabbit, The, 27
Giant Bones, The, 55
Giant Grummer's Christmas, 69
Giant Who Had No Heart in His
  Body, The, 27
Great Quillow, The, 29
Jack and the Beanstalk, 32

Molly and the Giant, 36
Molly Whipple, 36
Molly Whuppie, 36
Mop Servant, The, 37
Prince Loaf, 39
Pumpkin Giant, The, 83
Sneezy Snatcher and
  Sammy Small, 42
Three Golden Hairs of the King of
  the Cave Giants, The, 44
Three Little Pigs and the Ogre, The, 44
Ting-a-ling's Visit to Turilira, 45

GYPSIES

Gypsy Fiddle, The, 29
Gypsy in the Ghost House, The, 55
Jack and the Flock of Sheep, 31

Trapper's Tale of the First
  Birthday, The, 72

HOLIDAYS. See STORIES FOR HOLIDAY PROGRAMS, pp. 67–83

HUMOROUS STORIES

Ah Mee's Invention, 17
Cat and the Parrot, The, 20
Clever Peter and the Two
  Bottles, 36
Cow in the House, A, 11
Dancing Palm Tree, The, 49
Donkey and Scholars, 61
Donkey Egg, The, 23
Don't Count Your Chicks, 10
Doughnuts, The, 23
Ebenezer Never-Could-Sneezer, 24
Egg of Fortune, The, 9
Elephant's Child, The, 54
Emperor's New Clothes, The, 25
Finn M'Cool and the Giant
  Cucullin, 54
Five Chinese Brothers, The, 6
500 Hats of Bartholomew
  Cubbins, The, 6
Four Arrows, 55
Gardener, the Abbot, and the
  King, The, 33
Get Up and Bar the Door, 55
Giacco and His Bean, 15
Giant Grummer's Christmas, 69
Gone Is Gone, 31
Great Quillow, The, 29
Gudbrand on the Hillside, 29
Hereafterthis, 30
Herschel the Hero, 8
How Many Donkeys?, 30
How the Peasant Kept House, 31
Huckabuck Family, The, 82
Hudden and Dudden and Donald
  O'Neary, 31
Hungry Leprechaun, The, 81
Husband Who Wanted to Mind the
  House, The, 31

Husband Who Was to Mind the
  House, The, 31
I Know an Old Lady, 32
Invisible Silk Robe, The, 25
It Could Be Worse, 11
Jack and the Bean Tree, 32
King's Rijstepap, The, 33
Lad and the Fox, The, 10
Laughing Prince, The, 34
Lazy Jack, 34
Lazy Tok, 35
Lengthy, 8
Little Old Lady Who Swallowed a
  Fly, The, 32
Little Rooster and the Turkish
  Sultan, The, 35
Living in W'ales, 35
Mammo the Fool, 36
Mary, Mary, So Contrary!, 59
Master of All Masters, 36
Milkmaid and Her Pail, The, 9
Mr. Vinegar, 10
No Room, 11
Old One-Eye, 37
Otto and the Magic Potatoes, 38
Pedro de Malas Artes, or,
  Clumsy Pedro, 34
Presentneed, Bymeby, and
  Hereafter, 30
Prince Bertram the Bad, 12
Princess Who Could Not Cry, The, 39
Princess Whom No One Could
  Silence, The, 39
Proper Lesson for Those Who Would
  Burden Asses with Learning, A, 61
Pudding That Broke Up a
  Preaching, The, 83
Pumpkin Giant, The, 83

Shrewd Todie & Lyzer the Miser, 62
Shrovetide, 30
Soap, Soap, Soap!, 42
Squire's Bride, The, 42
Story of Ferdinand, The, 13
Sultan's Bath, The, 13
Talk, 63
Talking Cat, The, 43
Teeny-Tiny, 77
Three Sneezes, The, 44

Three Wishes, The, 14
Tikki Tikki Tembo, 45
Tony Di-Moany, 34
Too Much Nose, 61
Twist-Mouth Family, The, 15
What the Good Man Does Is Sure
    to Be Right, 29
When the Husband Stayed Home, 31
Wise Man on the Mountain, The, 11
Wonderful Tar-Baby, The, 48

JEWS

Mixed-up Feet and the Silly
    Bridegroom, The, 34
Shrewd Todie & Lyzer the Miser, 62

See also BIBLE STORIES; FOLKTALES—
Israel; FOLKTALES—Russia; JEWISH
HOLIDAYS; LEGENDS—Jewish

LEGENDS

American Indian
Angry Moon, The, 3
Fire Bringer, The, 25
Legend of Scarface, The, 58
Little Scar Face, 22
Nanabozho and the Wild Geese, 37
Ring in the Prairie, The, 40
'Twas in the Moon of Wintertime, 72
Zini and the Witches, 78

Chinese
Voice of the Great Bell, The, 63

Dutch
Dutch Boy and the Dike, The, 24

French
Clown of God, The, 69
Juggler of Notre Dame, The, 69
Story of Brother Johannick and His
    Silver Bell, The, 71

German
Legend of the Christmas Rose, The, 70
Pied Piper of Hamelin, The, 38

Italian
Bell of Atri, The, 18
Saint Francis and the Wolf, 41
Truce of the Wolf, The, 41
Wolf of Gubbio, The, 41

Jewish
King Solomon's Carpet, 33
Wise King and the Little Bee, The, 48

Medieval
Christmas at Greccio, 67
Franklin's Tale, The, 55
Gareth and Linette, 55
How Gareth of Orkney Won
    His Spurs, 55
King Arthur and His Sword, 57

Loathly Lady, The, 58
Phantom Knight of the Vandal
   Camp, The, 76
Sir Gawain and the Green Knight, 64
Sir Gawain and the Loathly Damsel, 58

North American
Baby Rainstorm, 51
Bold Dragoon, The, 74
Davy Crockett, 53
Joe Magarac, 56
John Henry, 57
Johnny Appleseed, 32
Legend of Sleepy Hollow, The, 76
Paul Bunyan, 60
Pecos Bill, 38
Rip Van Winkle, 62
Steel Driving Man, 57

Polish
Lullaby, 70

Roman
Cornelia's Jewels, 79
Horatius at the Bridge, 56

Russian
Babouscka, 67

Saints
Christmas at Greccio, 67
Joan of Arc, 56
Legend of St. Christopher, The, 70
Saint Francis and the Wolf, 41
Saint Patrick and the Last Snake, 81
Truce of the Wolf, The, 41
Wolf of Gubbio, The, 41

Spanish
Moor's Legacy, The, 59

Swiss
William Tell, 48

MODERN IMAGINATIVE STORIES

Ah Mee's Invention, 17
And We Are as We Are, 51
Andy and the Lion, 17
Animals' Peace Day, The, 3
Apple of Contentment, The, 51
Apple Tree, The, 73
Armadillo Who Had No Shell, The, 3
Bear's Toothache, The, 4
Bergamot, 52
Bertha Goldfoot, 52
Boy Who Discovered the
   Spring, The, 73
Brownies—Hush!, 68
Brownies—It's Christmas!, 67
Can Men Be Such Fools as All
   That?, 20
Caps for Sale, 10

Cat at Night, The, 5
Christmas Apple, The, 67
Christmas Cuckoo, The, 68
Christmas Eve in the Used Car Lot, 68
Christmas Promise, The, 68
Christmas That Was Nearly
   Lost, The, 68
Christmas Window, The, 68
Clever Peter and the Two Bottles, 36
Country Bunny and the Little Gold
   Shoes, The, 73
Craziest Hallowe'en, The, 75
Dancing Cow, The, 23
Dandelion, 5
Dragon and the Dragoon, The, 24
Easter Bunny That Overslept, The, 73
Ebenezer Never-Could-Sneezer, 23

Elephant and the Bad Baby, The, 6
Elephant's Child, The, 54
Elisabeth the Cow Ghost, 75
Elsie Piddock Skips in Her Sleep, 54
Emperor and the Kite, The, 25
Emperor's New Clothes, The, 25
Fierce Yellow Pumpkin, The, 75
Fifty-First Dragon, The, 54
Fir Tree, The, 69
Fisherman Under the Sea, The, 26
500 Hats of Bartholomew
   Cubbins, The, 6
Flagmakers, The, 80
Forest Full of Friends, The, 79
Frederick, 6
Frog of Roland, The, 55
Funny Thing, The, 6
Gears and Gasoline, 27
Georgie to the Rescue, 75
Giant Grummer's Christmas, 69
Gift, The, 69
Girl and the Goatherd, The, 28
Goblin Under the Stairs, The, 75
Golden Cobwebs, The, 69
Golden Egg Book, The, 73
Great Quillow, The, 29
Happy Prince, The, 56
Horace the Happy Ghost, 75
How Boots Befooled the King, 19
How Mrs. Santa Claus Saved
   Christmas, 69
How One Turned His Trouble to
   Some Account, 31
How the Camel Got His Hump, 30
How the Good Gifts Were Used
   by Two, 69
How the Princess's Pride Was
   Broken, 63
Huckabuck Family, The, 82
Hungry Leprechaun, The, 81
In the Forest, 8
In the Great Walled Country, 69
Inch by Inch, 8
Ittki Pittki, 32

Jenny's Birthday Book, 8
Jimmy Takes Vanishing Lessons, 32
Journey Cake, Ho!, 6
Journey on Eggs, 80
King of the Golden River, The, 57
King Stork, 33
Kingdom of the Greedy, The, 82
Knights of the Silver Shield, The, 57
Lengthy, 8
Lesson of Faith, A, 73
Little Bear, 8
Little Bear's Thanksgiving, 82
Little Daylight, 42
Little Dressmaker, The, 58
Little Engine That Could, The, 70
Little Green Elf's Christmas, The, 70
Little Match Girl, The, 79
Little Pagan Faun, The, 70
Little Piccola, 70
Little Toot, 9
Littlest Angel, The, 70
Living in W'ales, 35
Lonely Doll, The, 9
Lorax, The, 35
Lost Half-Hour, The, 58
Magic Feather Duster, The, 9
Magic Lollipop, The, 9
Man Who Lost His Head, The, 36
Many Moons, 36
May I Bring a Friend?, 9
Mighty Hunter, The, 9
Mike Mulligan and His Steam
   Shovel, 9
Millions of Cats, 10
Miss Suzy's Easter Surprise, 73
Mr. Brown and Mr. Gray, 10
Mr. Gumpy's Outing, 10
Mr. Rabbit and the Lovely Present, 79
Mousewife, The, 59
Murdoch's Rath, 81
My Grandfather Hendry Watty, 76
Night Before Christmas, The, 70
Nightingale, The, 60
Noël for Jeanne-Marie, 70

Nutcracker, The, 71
Old Man Rabbit's Thanksgiving
  Dinner, 82
One Dark Night, 76
One Thousand Christmas Beards, 71
Otto and the Magic Potatoes, 38
Paddy's Christmas, 71
Pelle's New Suit, 12
Peter and the Twelve-Headed
  Dragon, 24
Plain Princess, The, 38
Poor Count's Christmas, The, 71
Poppy Seed Cakes, The, 12
Prince and the Goose Girl, The, 61
Prince Bertram the Bad, 12
Princess and the Pea, The, 39
Princess Who Could Not Cry, The, 39
Princess with One
  Accomplishment, The, 61
Pumpkin Giant, The, 83
Puppy Who Wanted a Boy, The, 71
Quick-running Squash, A, 83
Rat-Catcher's Daughter, The, 40
Reluctant Dragon, The, 62
Remarkable Egg, The, 74
Richard Brown and the Dragon, 40
Rikki-Tikki-Tavi, 62
Rolling Rice Ball, The, 40
Rosie's Walk, 12
Runaway Sardine, The, 6
Selfish Giant, The, 74
Silver Hen, The, 71
Skillful Huntsman, The, 62
So-So Cat, The, 13
Space Witch, 77
Steadfast Tin Soldier, The, 43
Sugar Egg, The, 74
Surprise Party, The, 13
Swineherd, The, 63
Tailor of Gloucester, The, 71
Tale of Johnny Town-Mouse, The, 15
Tale of Peter Rabbit, The, 13
Tears of the Dragon, The, 43

Tell-Tale Heart, The, 63
Third Lamb, The, 71
Thousandth Gift, The, 64
Three Little Animals, 14
Three Little Pigs and the Ogre, The, 44
Tico and the Golden Wings, 15
Tilly Witch, 77
Tinder Box, The, 45
Ting-a-ling's Visit to Turilira, 45
Tomten, The, 15
Torten's Christmas Secret, 72
Trapper's Tale of the First
  Birthday, The, 72
Two of Everything, 46
Ugly Duckling, The, 46
Velveteen Rabbit, The, 74
Voyage of the Wee Red Cap, The, 72
Wee Christmas Cabin of
  Carn-na-ween, The, 72
Week of Sundays, A, 64
What Ailed the King, 64
What the Good Man Does Is Sure
  to Be Right, 29
What's in the Dark?, 15
When the Root Children Wake Up, 16
Where the Wild Things Are, 16
Whiskers of Ho Ho, The, 74
White Cat, The, 26
White Horse Girl and the Blue Wind
  Boy, The, 65
Who Took the Farmer's Hat?, 16
Why the Chimes Rang, 72
Wise Man on the Mountain, 11
Witch's Magic Cloth, The, 48
Wobble the Witch Cat, 78
Woggle of Witches, A, 78
Woman's Wit, 65
Wonderful Dragon of Timlin, The, 16
Wooden Shoes of Little Wolff, The, 72
Woodman and the Goblins, The, 78
Worker in Sandalwood, The, 72
World in the Candy Egg, The, 74

MODERN REALISTIC STORIES

Abraham Lincoln, 80
Angelo, the Naughty One, 3
Appolonia's Valentine, 81
Baker's Daughter, The, 18
Beany and His New Recorder, 18
Better Than a Parade, 80
Betty Zane, Heroine of Fort Henry, 52
Bidushka Lays an Easter Egg, 73
Blueberries for Sal, 4
Cheese, Peas, and Chocolate
   Pudding, 5
Columbus, 80
Cosette's Christmas, 68
Cranberry Thanksgiving, 82
Don't Count Your Chicks, 10
Doughnuts, The, 23
Down down the Mountain, 5
Edie Changes Her Mind, 5
Egg Tree, The, 73
First Thanksgiving, The, 82
George Washington, 80
Grace Bedell and Lincoln's Beard,
   Why the President Wore
   Whiskers, 81
Herschel the Hero, 8
In Clean Hay, 69
Indians for Thanksgiving, 82
Jack-o'-Lantern, The, 75
Jack-o'-Lantern Witch, The, 75
Joan of Arc, 56
Juan Brings a Valentine, 82
Juanita, 73
Little Blind Shepherd, The, 70
Little House, The, 8
Madeline, 9

Maid and Her Pail of Milk, The, 10
Make Way for Ducklings, 9
Mama and the Graduation Present, 79
Mei Li, 79
My Mother and I, 79
Mysterious Gold and Purple
   Box, The, 37
Pelle's New Suit, 12
Peterkins Celebrate the
   "Fourth," The, 81
Play with Me, 12
Plymouth Thanksgiving, The, 82
Pumpkinseeds, 12
Rain, Rain Rivers, 12
Ride on the Wind, 62
Ring in the New!, 80
Roll-Call of the Reef, The, 77
Rosa-Too-Little, 12
Sam, 12
Silent Night, the Story of a Song, 71
Smoke, 13
Snowy Day, The, 13
Star for Hansi, A, 71
Star-Spangled Banner Girl, 81
Story About Ping, The, 13
Story of Pancho and the Bull with the
   Crooked Tail, The, 13
Sunflowers for Tina, 13
Talking Cat, The, 43
Thankful, 83
Valentine Box, The, 82
Wait for William, 15
Where Love Is, There God Is Also, 72
Whistle for Willie, 16

MUSIC STORIES

Beany and His New Recorder, 18
Gypsy Fiddle, The, 29
Hansel and Gretel, 29

I Know an Old Lady, 32
Nutcracker, The, 71
Peter and the Wolf, 38

Silent Night, the Story of a Song, 71
Sing for Christmas, 71

Sorcerer's Apprentice, The, 42
'Twas in the Moon of Wintertime, 72

MYTHS

American Indian
How Animals Brought Fire to Man, 25
Stealing the Springtime, 74
Why Women Talk More than Men, 65

Greek
Cupid and Psyche, 81
Daedalus and Icarus, 53
Golden Fleece, The, 55
Golden Touch, The, 28
Miraculous Pitcher, The, 59
Pegasus, 60
Persephone and Demeter, 73
Perseus, 60
Phaeton, 61

Search for the Golden Fleece, The, 55
Theseus, 64

Norse
Apples of Iduna, The, 58
Apples of Youth, The, 58
Baldur, 51
Contest with the Giants, A, 64
How Thor's Hammer Was Lost and
    Found, 56
Loki . . . Apples of Youth, 58
Thor and Loki in the Giants' City, 64
Thor and the Giant King, 64
Thor . . . How the Thunderer Was
    Tricked, 64
Thor's Unlucky Journey, 64

REPETITIVE STORIES. *See* CUMULATIVE AND REPETITIVE STORIES

SAINTS. *See* LEGENDS—Saints

STORIES BY COUNTRY

*Africa**
Mysterious Gold and Purple
    Box, The, 37

Austria
Third Lamb, The, 71

Canada
Talking Cat, The, 43
Worker in Sandalwood, The, 72

China
Ah Mee's Invention, 17
Emperor and the Kite, The, 25
Five Chinese Brothers, The, 6
Ma Lien and the Magic Brush, 35
Mei Li, 79
Story About Ping, The, 13
Whiskers of Ho Ho, The, 74

Czechoslovakia
Bidushka Lays an Easter Egg, 73

*See p. x for an explanation of this
classification.

England
Elsie Piddock Skips in Her Sleep, 54
Tailor of Gloucester, The, 71

France
Cosette's Christmas, 68
Joan of Arc, 56
Last Lesson in French, The, 57
Madeline, 9
Wooden Shoes of Little Wolff, The, 72

Germany
Bertha Goldfoot, 52
Christmas Apple, The, 67
Frog of Roland, The, 55
Star for Hansi, A, 71

India
Foolish, Timid Rabbit, The, 7
Stolen Necklace, The, 13, 28
Tico and the Golden Wings, 15
Tot Botot and His Little Flute, 15

Ireland
Hungry Leprechaun, The, 81
St. Patrick and the Last Snake, 81
Voyage of the Wee Red Cap, The, 72
Wee Christmas Cabin of
   Carn-na-ween, The, 72
Week of Sundays, A, 64

Japan
Fisherman Under the Sea, The, 26
Rolling Rice Ball, The, 40
Tears of the Dragon, The, 43
Witch's Magic Cloth, The, 48

Mexico
Angelo, the Naughty One, 3
Story of Pancho and the Bull with the
   Crooked Tail, The, 13

Poland
In Clean Hay, 69

Portugal
Gift, The, 69

Russia
Where Love Is, There God Is Also, 72

Spain
Christmas Promise, The, 68
Story of Ferdinand, The, 13

Sweden
Pelle's New Suit, 12

United States of America (regional)
      AMERICAN INDIAN
Mighty Hunter, The, 9

      PENNSYLVANIA DUTCH
Appolonia's Valentine, 81
Egg Tree, The, 73

      SOUTHERN MOUNTAINS
Down down the Mountain, 5

      SOUTHWEST
Juanita, 73

TALL TALES. See LEGENDS—North America

TOYS

Corduroy, 5
Little Engine That Could, The, 70

Lonely Doll, The, 9
Velveteen Rabbit, The, 74

WITCHES AND WIZARDS

Aniello, 17

Baba Yaga, 18

Bergamot, 52

Craziest Hallowe'en, The, 75

Hansel and Gretel, 29

Hungry Old Witch, The, 75

Jack-o'-Lantern Witch, The, 75

Jorinda and Joringel, 57

King Stork, 33

Magic Ball, The, 76

Mountain Witch and the
  Peddler, The, 76

Old Hag of the Forest, The, 81

Old Witch, The, 76

Peter and the Witch of the Wood, 76

So-So Cat, The, 13

Sorcerer's Apprentice, The, 42

Space Witch, 77

Tamara and the Sea Witch, 43

Tilly Witch, 77

Vasilisa the Beautiful, 22

Which Was Witch?, 78

Witches' Ride, The, 78

Witch's Magic Cloth, The, 48

Wobble the Witch Cat, 78

Woggle of Witches, A, 78

Zini and the Witches, 78

Alphabetical List of Stories

Abraham Lincoln, 80
Adventure of My Grandfather, The, 74
Adventurous Mouse, The, 3
Ah Mee's Invention, 17
Aladdin; or, The Wonderful Lamp, 17
Ali Baba and the Forty Thieves, 26
All in the Morning Early, 3
Alligator and the Jackal, The, 32
And We Are as We Are, 51
Androcles and the Lion, 17
Andy and the Lion, 17
Angelo, the Naughty One, 3
Angry Moon, The, 3
Angus and the Ducks, 3
Aniello, 17
Animal Musicians, The, 4
Animals' Peace Day, The, 3
Anklet of Jewels, The, 21
Apple of Contentment, The, 51
Apple Tree, The, 73
Apples of Iduna, The, 58
Apples of Youth, The, 58
Appolonia's Valentine, 81
Argonauts, The, 55
Armadillo Who Had No Shell, The, 3
As the World Pays, 44
Aschenputtel, 22
Ashputtel, 21
Ask Mr. Bear, 3

At the Seder, 78
Away Went Wolfgang!, 3
Baba Yaga, 18
Baba Yaga and the Little Girl with the
   Kind Heart, 18
Babouscka, 67
Baboushka and the Three Kings, 67
Baby Rainstorm, 51
Baker's Daughter, The, 18
Balder and the Mistletoe, 51
Baldpate, 18
Baldur, 51
Baldur, the Beautiful, 51
Baldur's Doom, 51
Ballad of the Harp Weaver, The, 51
Ballad of William Sycamore, The, 52
Baucis and Philemon, 59
Beany and His New Recorder, 18
Bear's Toothache, The, 4
Beautiful Blue Jay, The, 18
Beauty and the Beast, 18
Bedtime for Frances, 4
Beetle, 18
Beggar Boy and the Fox, The, 40
Bell of Atri, The, 18
Belling the Cat, 9
Bellerophon, 60
Beowulf, 52
Beowulf and the Fire Dragon, 52

Bergamot, 52
Bertha Goldfoot, 52
Betrothal Feast, The, 52
Better Than a Parade, 80
Betty Zane, Heroine of Fort Henry, 52
Bidushka Lays an Easter Egg, 73
Bigger Giant, The, 54
Billy Beg and the Bull, 18
Billy Goat in the Chili Patch, The, 4
Birth of Jesus, The, 67
Blabbermouth, 19
Black Magic, 19
Blind Man and the Deaf Man, The, 19
Blind Man, the Deaf Man, and the
    Donkey, The, 19
Blind Men and the Elephant, The, 19
Blue Rose, The, 52
Blueberries for Sal, 4
Bold Dragoon, The, 74
Boots and His Brothers, 19
Boy Who Cried Wolf, The, 4
Boy Who Discovered the
    Spring, The, 73
Boy Who Drew Cats, The, 19
Boy Who Stopped the Sea, The, 24
Boy Without a Name, The, 19
Brahman, the Tiger, and the Six
    Judges, The, 44
Brave Little Tailor, The, 20
Bremen Town Musicians, The, 4
Briar Rose, 42
Bride for the Sea God, A, 52
Broad Man, the Tall Man, and the Man
    with Eyes of Flame, The, 58
Brownies—Hush!, 68
Brownies—It's Christmas!, 67
Budulinek, 20
Bun, The, 6
Bundle of Sticks, A, 4
Buried Moon, The, 74
Buried Treasure, The, 20
Burning of the Rice Fields, The, 20
Can Men Be Such Fools as All That?, 20
Cap o' Rushes, 22

Caps for Sale, 10
Cat and the Parrot, The, 20
Cat at Night, The, 5
Catskin, 22
Catskins, 22
Cenerentola, 22
Champion of Ireland, The, 63
Chanina and the Angels, 21
Chanticleer, 21
Chanticleer and the Fox, 21
Cheese, Peas, and Chocolate
    Pudding, 5
Chien-Nang, 52
Child in the Bamboo Grove, The, 21
Childe Rowland, 52
Childe Rowland and the King of
    Elfland, 52
Children of Lir, The, 53
Chimaera, The, 60
Christmas Apple, The, 67
Christmas at Greccio, 67
Christmas Cuckoo, The, 68
Christmas Eve in the Used Car Lot, 68
Christmas Promise, The, 68
Christmas Spider, The, 68
Christmas That Was Nearly
    Lost, The, 68
Christmas Visitors, The, 68
Christmas Window, The, 68
Chu Cuoi's Trip to the Moon, 21
Cinderella, 21
Circus Baby, The, 5
Clever Manka, 53
Clever Peasant Girl, The, 53
Clever Peter and the Two Bottles, 36
Clever Prince, The, 53
Clever Turtle, The, 22
Clever Wife, The, 22
Clown of God, The, 69
Cobbler, The, 20
Cock, the Mouse, and the Little Red
    Hen, The, 5
Columbus, 80
Columbus and the Egg, 80

Conjure Wives, The, 75
Contest with the Giants, A, 64
Corduroy, 5
Cornelia, 79
Cornelia's Jewels, 79
Cosette's Christmas, 68
Country Bunny and the Little Gold
  Shoes, The, 73
Cow in the House, A, 11
Cow-Tail Switch, The, 53
Cranberry Thanksgiving, 82
Craziest Hallowe'en, The, 75
Crochera, The, 27
Crocodile's Tale, A, 5
Crumb in His Beard, A, 23
Cruse of Oil—165 B.C., The, 78
Cupid and Psyche, 81
Curious George Takes a Job, 5
Daedalus, 53
Daedalus and Icarus, 53
Dance of the Animals, 23
Dancing Cow, The, 23
Dancing Palm Tree, The, 49
Dandelion, 5
Daniel in the Den of Lions, 23
Daniel in the Lions' Den, 23
Daniel, the Brave Young Captive, 23
David and Goliath, 53
Davy Crockett, 53
Death of Balder, The, 51
Demeter and Persephone, 73
Dick Whittington and His Cat, 23
Diverting Adventures of Tom
  Thumb, The, 45
Doctor and Detective Too, 23
Doctor Know-All, 23
Doctor Know-It-All, 23
Donal O'Ciaran from Connaught, 20
Donkey and Scholars, 61
Donkey Egg, The, 23
Donkey Which Made Gold, The, 34
Don't Count Your Chicks, 10
Doughnuts, The, 23
Down down the Mountain, 5

Dragon and His Grandmother, The, 24
Dragon and the Dragoon, The, 24
Dragonmaster, 24
Drakesbill and His Friends, 5
Drakestail, 5
Dutch Boy and the Dike, The, 24
Dwarf and the Cobbler's Sons, The, 68
Earth Gnome, The, 24
East of the Sun and West of the
  Moon, 24
Easter Bunny That Overslept, The, 73
Ebenezer Never-Could-Sneezer, 24
Edie Changes Her Mind, 5
Egg of Fortune, The, 9
Egg Tree, The, 73
Eggs, The, 65
8,000 Stones, 24
Elephant and the Bad Baby, The, 6
Elephant's Child, The, 54
Elisabeth the Cow Ghost, 75
Elsie Piddock Skips in Her Sleep, 54
Elves and the Shoemaker, The, 68
Emperor and the Kite, The, 25
Emperor's New Clothes, The, 25
End of the World, The, 7
Endless Tale, The, 43
Escape of the Animals, The, 25
Esther . . . Who Saved Her People, 78
Extraordinary Tug-of-War, The, 45
False Friend, The, 25
Farmer and the King, The, 25
Fat Cat, The, 21
Feather o' My Wing, 54
Fierce Yellow Pumpkin, The, 75
Fifty-First Dragon, The, 54
Fifty Red Night-Caps, 10
Fin M'Coul and Cucullin, 54
Finn M'Cool and the Giant
  Cucullin, 54
Finn McCoul, 54
Fir Tree, The, 69
Fire Bringer, The, 25
First Thanksgiving, The, 82
Fisherman and His Wife, The, 25

Fisherman and the Genie, The, 54
Fisherman and the Goblet, The, 54
Fisherman Under the Sea, The, 26
Five Chinese Brothers, The, 6
500 Hats of Bartholomew
  Cubbins, The, 6
Five Queer Brothers, The, 6
Flagmakers, The, 80
Flea, The, 26
Flight of Icarus, The, 53
Flood and Noah's Ark, The, 11
Flying Ship, The, 26
Folly of Panic, The, 7
Fool of the World and the Flying
  Ship, The, 26
Foolish, Timid Rabbit, The, 7
Forest Bride, The, 26
Forest Full of Friends, The, 79
Forty Thieves, The, 26
Four Arrows, 55
Four Musicians, The, 4
Fox and the Crow, The, 21
Franklin's Tale, The, 55
Frederick, 6
Frog, The, 55
Frog of Roland, The, 55
Frog Prince, The, 27
From Tiger to Anansi, 27
Funny Little Woman, The, 27
Funny Thing, The, 6
Gallant Tailor, The, 20
Gardener, the Abbot, and the
  King, The, 33
Gareth and Linette, 55
Gears and Gasoline, 27
George Washington, 80
George Washington and His
  Hatchet, 80
Georgie to the Rescue, 75
Get Up and Bar the Door, 55
Ghost Dog of South Mountain, The, 75
Ghost Who Was Afraid of Being
  Bagged, The, 27
Giacco and His Bean, 15

Giant and the Dwarf, The, 27
Giant and the Rabbit, The, 27
Giant Bones, The, 55
Giant Grummer's Christmas, 69
Giant Who Had No Heart in His
  Body, The, 27
Gift, The, 69
Gift from the Heart, A, 28
Gifts for the First Birthday, 72
Gingerbread Boy, The, 6
Gingerbread Man, The, 6
Girl and the Goatherd, The, 28
Girl Monkey and the String of
  Pearls, The, 28
Girl Who Could Think, The, 28
Goat Well, The, 28
Goblin Under the Stairs, The, 75
Golden Apple, The, 7
Golden Cobwebs, The, 69
Golden Egg Book, The, 73
Golden Fish, The, 25
Golden Fleece, The, 55
Golden Goose, The, 28
Golden Gourd, The, 28
Golden Lynx, The, 28
Golden Phoenix, The, 55
Golden Touch, The, 28
Golden Touch of King Midas, The, 28
Gone Is Gone, 31
Good Night, Owl!, 7
Goose Hans, 34
Gorgon's Head, The, 60
Grace Bedell and Lincoln's Beard, Why
  the President Wore Whiskers, 81
Grandmother Marta, 29
Grandmother's Tale, 78
Grateful Beasts, The, 29
Graylegs, 61
Great Big Enormous Turnip, The, 15
Great Miracle, A, 78
Great Quillow, The, 29
Grendel, 52
Grendel the Monster, 52
Gudbrand on the Hillside, 29

Guest for Halll, A, 29
Guinea Pig's Tale, The, 7
Gunniwolf, The, 7
Gunny Wolf, The, 7
Gypsy Fiddle, The, 29
Gypsy in the Ghost House, The, 55
Half-Chick, The, 7
Hammer of Thor, The, 56
Hans in Luck, 29
Hansel and Gretel, 29
Happy-Go-Lucky, 29
Happy Lion, The, 7
Happy Prince, The, 56
Hardy Tin Soldier, The, 43
Hare and the Hedgehog, The, 30
Harry the Dirty Dog, 7
Henny-Penny, 7
Hereafterthis, 30
Hero of Haarlem, The, 24
Herschel the Hero, 8
Highwayman, The, 56
Hobyahs, The, 75
Horace the Happy Ghost, 75
Horatius at the Bridge, 56
Horse-Egg, The, 23
House That Jack Built, The, 8
How a Poor Man Was Rewarded, 30
How Animals Brought Fire to Man, 25
How Boots Befooled the King, 19
How Gareth of Orkney Won His
  Spurs, 55
How Horatius Held the Bridge, 56
How Many Donkeys?, 30
How Mrs. Santa Claus Saved
  Christmas, 69
How One Turned His Trouble to
  Some Account, 31
How Pecos Bill Won and Lost His
  Bouncing Bride, 38
How Perseus Slew the Gorgon, 60
How Phaeton Drove the Horses of
  the Sun, 61
How Spider Got a Thin Waist, 30
How the Camel Got His Hump, 30

How the Camel Got His Proud
  Look, 30
How the Dog Became the Servant
  of Man, 30
How the Good Gifts Were Used
  by Two, 69
How the Hare Told the Truth About
  His Horse, 30
How the Manx Cat Lost Its Tail, 30
How the Peasant Kept House, 31
How the Porcupine Outwitted the
  Fox, 31
How the Princess's Pride Was
  Broken, 63
How the Robin's Breast Became
  Red, 31
How the Siamese Cats Got the Kink
  in the End of Their Tails, 31
How Thor Found His Hammer, 56
How Thor's Hammer Was Lost and
  Found, 56
How to Tell a Real Princess, 39
How to Weigh an Elephant, 25
Huckabuck Family, The, 82
Hudden and Dudden and Donald
  O'Neary, 31
Hungry Leprechaun, The, 81
Hungry Old Witch, The, 75
Hungry Spider and the Turtle, 31
Husband Who Wanted to Mind the
  House, The, 31
Husband Who Was to Mind the
  House, The, 31
I Am Your Misfortune, 31
I Cannot Tell a Lie, 80
I Know an Old Lady, 32
Ifrit and the Magic Gifts, The, 32
I'm Going on a Bear Hunt, 8
Impudent Bee, The, 48
In Clean Hay, 69
In the Forest, 8
In the Great Walled Country, 69
Inch by Inch, 8
Indians for Thanksgiving, 82

Invisible Silk Robe, The, 25
Issun Boshi, the Inchling, 45
It Could Be Worse, 11
Ittki Pittki, 32
Jack and His Comrades, 4
Jack and the Bean Tree, 32
Jack and the Beanstalk, 32
Jack and the Flock of Sheep, 31
Jack and the Friendly Animals, 4
Jack and the North West Wind, 34
Jack and the Robbers, 4
Jack and the Varmints, 20
Jack-o'-Lantern, The, 75
Jack-o'-Lantern Witch, The, 75
Jackal and the Alligator, The, 32
Jason, 55
Jeanne d'Arc, 56
Jenny's Birthday Book, 8
Jesper Who Herded the Hares, 41
Jesus, 67
Jeweled Slipper, The, 22
Jimmy Takes Vanishing Lessons, 32
Joan of Arc, 56
Joco and the Fishbone, 32
Joe Magarac, 56
Joe Magarac and His U.S.A.
  Citizen Papers, 56
John Henry, 57
Johnny Appleseed, 32
Johnny-Cake, 6
Jolly Tailor Who Became King, The, 32
Jorinda and Joringel, 57
Joseph and His Brothers, 33
Journey Cake, Ho!, 6
Journey on Eggs, 80
Juan Brings a Valentine, 82
Juanita, 73
Juggler of Notre Dame, The, 69
Kari Woodengown, 22
Katcha and the Devil, 76
Keel-Wee, a Korean Rip Van
  Winkle, 62
Keloğlan and the Ooh-Genie, 34
Kindai and the Ape, 17

King and the Shepherd, The, 33
King Arthur, 57
King Arthur and His Sword, 57
King Clothes, 29
King John and the Abbot of
  Canterbury, 33
King o' the Cats, The, 76
King of the Birds, The, 8
King of the Golden River, The, 57
King Solomon's Carpet, 33
King Stork, 33
King Thrushbeard, 61
Kingdom of the Greedy, The, 82
King's Choice, The, 8
King's Rijstepap, The, 33
Kiss from the Beautiful Fiorita, A, 57
Knights of the Silver Shield, The, 57
Kojata, 33
Kuratko the Terrible, 21
Lad and the Fox, The, 10
Lad Who Went to the North
  Wind, The, 33
Lairdie with the Heart of Gold, The, 57
Laird's Lass and the Gobha's
  Son, The, 57
Lamb with the Golden Fleece, The, 28
Last Lesson, The, 57
Last Lesson in French, The, 57
Laughing Prince, The, 34
Lazy Jack, 34
Lazy Tok, 35
Leak in the Dike, The, 24
Legend of Babouscka, The, 67
Legend of St. Christopher, The, 70
Legend of Scarface, The, 58
Legend of Sleepy Hollow, The, 76
Legend of the Christmas Rose, The, 70
Legend of the Orange
  Princess, The, 35
Legend of the Willow Plate, The, 58
Legs of the Moon, The, 35
Lengthy, 8
Lesson of Faith, A, 73
Lion and the Mouse, The, 8

Lion and the Rat, The, 8
Little Alligator and the Jackal, The, 32
Little Bear, 8
Little Bear's Thanksgiving, 82
Little Blind Shepherd, The, 70
Little Clock-Maker, The, 67
Little Cockerel, The, 35
Little Daylight, 42
Little Dressmaker, The, 58
Little Engine That Could, The, 70
Little Green Elf's Christmas, The, 70
Little Hatchy Hen, 8
Little Hero of Haarlem, The, 24
Little House, The, 8
Little Juggler, The, 69
Little Match Girl, The, 79
Little Old Lady Who Swallowed a
    Fly, The, 32
Little One-Eye, Little Two-Eyes, and
    Little Three-Eyes, 37
Little Pagan Faun, The, 70
Little Piccola, 70
Little Rooster and the Diamond
    Button, The, 35
Little Rooster and the Turkish
    Sultan, The, 35
Little Rooster, the Diamond Button,
    and the Turkish Sultan, The, 35
Little Scar Face, 22
Little Scarred One, The, 22
Little Sister and the Zimwi, 47
Little Toot, 9
Little White Hen, The, 9
Littlest Angel, The, 70
Living in W'ales, 35
Loathly Lady, The, 58
Loki . . . Apples of Youth, 58
Lonely Doll, The, 9
Long, Broad, & Quickeye, 58
Long, Broad, and Sharpsight, 58
Long Leather Bag, The, 76
Longshanks, Girth, and Keen, 58
Look, There Is a Turtle Flying, 46
Lorax, The, 35

Lost Half-Hour, The, 58
Love like Salt, 58
Lullaby, 70
Ma Liang and His Magic Brush, 35
Ma Lien and the Magic Brush, 35
Madam Crab Loses Her Head, 35
Madeline, 9
Magic Ball, The, 76
Magic Bottles, The, 35
Magic Box, The, 58
Magic Crystal, The, 54
Magic Dumplings, The, 47
Magic Feather Duster, The, 9
Magic Lollipop, The, 9
Magic Mortar, The, 47
Magic Tree, The, 36
Magical Crock, The, 35
Magician, The, 78
Maid and Her Pail of Milk, The, 10
Maiden with the Black Wooden
    Bowl, The, 59
Maiden with the Wooden
    Helmet, The, 59
Make Way for Ducklings, 9
Mama and the Graduation Present, 79
Mammo the Fool, 36
Man o' the Clan, The, 59
Man Who Didn't Believe in
    Ghosts, The, 59
Man Who Lost His Head, The, 36
Man Who Walked Widdershins
    round the Kirk, The, 59
Many Moons, 36
Mare at the Wedding, The, 42
Marvel of the Sword, The, 57
Mary, Mary, So Contrary!, 59
Master Kho and the Tiger, 44
Master of All Masters, 36
Matter of Mathematics, A, 62
May I Bring a Friend?, 9
Meeting of the Young Mice, The, 9
Mei Li, 79
Midas, 28
Mighty Hunter, The, 9

Mighty Mikko, 39
Mike Mulligan and His Steam
  Shovel, 9
Milkmaid and Her Pail, The, 9
Mill at the Bottom of the Sea, The, 48
Miller-King, The, 40
Millions of Cats, 10
Minotaur, The, 64
Miraculous Pitcher, The, 59
Mirza and the Ghul, 36
Miss Suzy's Easter Surprise, 73
Mr. Brown and Mr. Gray, 10
Mr. Gumpy's Outing, 10
Mr. Rabbit and Mr. Bear, 36
Mr. Rabbit and the Lovely Present, 79
Mr. Vinegar, 10
Mitten, The, 10
Mixed-up Feet and the Silly
  Bridegroom, The, 34
Molly and the Giant, 36
Molly Whipple, 36
Molly Whuppie, 36
Monastery of No Cares, The, 37
Monkey and the Crocodile, The, 37
Monkeys and the Little Red
  Hats, The, 10
Monkey's Pomegranate, The, 11
Moon Princess, The, 37
Moor's Legacy, The, 59
Mop Servant, The, 37
Morgan and the Pot of Brains, 59
Moses Delivers the People of Israel, 37
Moses in the Bulrushes, 10
Mountain Witch and the
  Peddler, The, 76
Mouse Bride, The, 26
Mouse-Princess, The, 26
Mousewife, The, 59
Murdoch's Rath, 81
Musicians of Bremen, The, 4
My Grandfather Hendry Watty, 76
My Mother and I, 79
My Mother Is the Most Beautiful
  Woman in the World, 79

Mysterious Gold and Purple
  Box, The, 37
Nail Soup, 43
Namalah and the Magic Carpet, 33
Nanabozho and the Wild Geese, 37
Nanny Who Wouldn't Go Home
  to Supper, 11
Nazar the Brave, 20
Neighbors, The, 10
Nibble Nibble Mousekin, 29
Night Before Christmas, The, 70
Nightingale, The, 60
No Room, 11
Noah and the Ark, 11
Noël for Jeanne-Marie, 70
Nomi and the Magic Fish, 22
Nose, The, 61
Nutcracker, The, 71
Of King Arthur, 57
Ogre, the Sun, and the Raven, The, 37
Old Acquaintance Is Soon Forgot!, 37
Old Dame and Her Silver
  Sixpence, The, 11
Old Gally Mander, 76
Old Hag of the Forest, The, 81
Old Man Rabbit's Thanksgiving
  Dinner, 82
Old One-Eye, 37
Old Witch, The, 76
Old Woman and Her
  Dumpling, The, 27
Old Woman and Her Pig, The, 11
Old Woman and the Fish, The, 14
Old Woman and the Tramp, The, 43
Old Woman Who Lived in a
  Vinegar Bottle, The, 25
Once a Mouse, 11
One Dark Night, 76
One-Eye, Two-Eyes, and
  Three-Eyes, 37
One Fine Day, 11
One for the Price of Two, 37
One Silver Second, 12
One Thousand Christmas Beards, 71

One Who Wasn't Afraid, The, 37
Orange Tree King, The, 40
Oté, 38
Otto and the Magic Potatoes, 38
Our Lady's Juggler, 69
Outside Cat, The, 12
Owl and the Woodpecker, The, 12
Paddy's Christmas, 71
Painted Eyebrow, The, 60
Pancake, The, 6
Pancakes and Pies, 35
Parrot of Limo Verde, The, 38
Parson and the Clerk, The, 33
Partnership of Rabbit and Elephant,
  and What Came of It, The, 38
Patrick O'Donnell and the
  Leprechaun, 81
Paul Bunyan, 60
Pecos Bill, 38
Peddler of Ballaghadereen, The, 81
Pedro de Malas Artes, or, Clumsy
  Pedro, 34
Pegasus, 60
Pekka and the Rogues, 47
Pelle's New Suit, 12
Per and the North Wind, 34
Persephone and Demeter, 73
Persephone and the Springtime, 73
Perseus, 60
Peter and the Twelve-Headed
  Dragon, 24
Peter and the Witch of the Wood, 76
Peter and the Wolf, 38
Peter Ox, 38
Peter, Paul, and Espen Cinderlad, 19
Peterkins Celebrate the
  "Fourth," The, 81
Phaeton, 61
Phantom Knight of the Vandal
  Camp, The, 76
Pied Piper, The, 38
Pied Piper of Franchville, The, 38
Pied Piper of Hamelin, The, 38
Pig-headed Wife, The, 59

Plain Princess, The, 38
Play with Me, 12
Plymouth Thanksgiving, The, 82
Pomegranate Seeds, The, 73
Poor Count's Christmas, The, 71
Poppy Seed Cakes, The, 12
Pottle o' Brains, A, 59
Presentneed, Bymeby, and
  Hereafter, 30
Priceless Cats, The, 23
Prince and the Goose Girl, The, 61
Prince Bertram the Bad, 12
Prince Loaf, 39
Princess and the Pea, The, 39
Princess and the Vagabone, The, 61
Princess of Light, The, 21
Princess of the Full Moon, 61
Princess of the Mountain, The, 39
Princess of the Rice Fields, The, 39
Princess of Tomboso, The, 61
Princess on the Glass Hill, The, 39
Princess on the Glass
  Mountain, The, 39
Princess Who Could Not Cry, The, 39
Princess Whom No One Could
  Silence, The, 39
Princess with One
  Accomplishment, The, 61
Princess with the Golden
  Shoes, The, 46
Proper Lesson for Those Who Would
  Burden Asses with Learning, A, 61
Proserpina and the Pomegranate
  Seeds, 73
Prudent Hans, 34
Pudding That Broke Up a
  Preaching, The, 83
Pumpkin Giant, The, 83
Pumpkinseeds, 12
Puppy Who Wanted a Boy, The, 71
Puss in Boots, 39
Quarrel, The, 40
Quick-running Squash, A, 83
Rabbit and the Clay Man, The, 49

Race Between Hare and
Hedgehog, The, 30
Rags-and-Tatters, 40
Rain, Rain Rivers, 12
Rapunzel, 40
Rat-Catcher's Daughter, The, 40
Ratcatcher of Hamelin, The, 38
Real Princess, The, 39
Red-Chicken, 5
Reluctant Dragon, The, 62
Remarkable Egg, The, 74
Resurrection, The, 74
Richard Brown and the Dragon, 40
Ride on the Wind, 62
Rikki-Tikki-Tavi, 62
Ring in the New!, 80
Ring in the Prairie, The, 40
Rip Van Winkle, 62
Robin Hood and the Golden Arrow, 62
Roland and Oliver, 62
Roland for an Oliver, A, 62
Roll-Call of the Reef, The, 77
Rolling Rice Ball, The, 40
Rooster and the Hen, The, 11
Rosa-Too-Little, 12
Rosie's Walk, 12
Rumpelstiltskin, 40
Runaway Bunny, The, 12
Runaway Sardine, The, 6
Rustem and Sohrab, 63
Sabot of Little Wolff, The, 72
Sack of Truth, The, 41
Sacred Amulet, The, 41
St. Francis and the First Christmas
Crèche, 67
Saint Francis and the Wolf, 41
Saint Patrick and the Last Snake, 81
Salt, 41
Sam, 12
Sandy MacNeil and His Dog, 62
Scarface, 58
Schippeitaro, 77
Schnitzle, Schnotzle, Schnootzle, 68
Search for the Golden Fleece, The, 55

Search for the Magic Lake, The, 41
Selfish Giant, The, 74
Seven at a Blow, 20
Seven Simeons, The, 26
Seven Simons, The, 26
Seven-Year Blessing, The, 41
Sheep and the Pig That Built the
House, The, 4
Shepherd's Boy, 4
Ship That Sailed by Land and
Sea, The, 26
Shoemaker and the Elves, The, 68
Shooting Match at Nottingham
Town, The, 62
Shrewd Todie & Lyzer the Miser, 62
Shrovetide, 30
Silent Night, the Story of a Song, 71
Silly Goose War, The, 19
Silly Jean, 34
Silver Hen, The, 71
Silver Penny, The, 41
Sing for Christmas, 71
Sir Gawain and the Green Knight, 64
Sir Gawain and the Loathly Damsel, 58
Sixty at a Blow, 20
Skillful Huntsman, The, 62
Sky Bright Axe/Paul Bunyan, The, 60
Sleeping Beauty, The, 41
Slip! Slop! Gobble!, 21
Smoke, 13
Sneezy Snatcher and Sammy
Small, 42
Snegourka, the Snow Maiden, 42
Snow Maiden, The, 42
Snow White and the Seven Dwarfs, 42
Snowdrop, 42
Snowflake, 42
Snowy Day, The, 13
Soap, Soap, Soap!, 42
Sody Sallyraytus, 14
Sohrab and Rustem, 63
Song of Beowulf, The, 52
Sorcerer's Apprentice, The, 42
So-So Cat, The, 13

Soul of the Great Bell, The, 63
Space Witch, 77
Squire's Bride, The, 42
Star for Hansi, A, 71
Star-Spangled Banner Girl, 81
Start with Something Sweet, 78
Steadfast Tin Soldier, The, 43
Stealing the Springtime, 74
Steel Driving Man, 57
Steelmaker/Joe Magarac, 56
Stolen Necklace, The, 13, 28
Stone Lion, The, 63
Stone Soup, 43
Story, a Story, A, 43
Story About Ping, The, 13
Story of Ala-ed-din; or, The
  Wonderful Lamp, 17
Story of Balder, The, 51
Story of Brother Johannick and His
  Silver Bell, The, 71
Story of Chicken-Licken, The, 7
Story of Ferdinand, The, 13
Story of Pancho and the Bull with the
  Crooked Tail, The, 13
Story of Perseus, The, 60
Story of the Fisherman, The, 54
Story of the Stone Lion, The, 63
Story of the Three Bears, The, 14
Story of the Three Little Pigs, The, 14
Storyteller, The, 43
Strange Visitor, The, 77
Stubborn Sillies, The, 55
Succos, 79
Sugar Egg, The, 74
Sultan's Bath, The, 13
Sunflowers for Tina, 13
Surprise Party, The, 13
Swan Children, The, 53
Swineherd, The, 63
Sword in the Stone, The, 57
Tailor of Gloucester, The, 71
Tale of a Black Cat, The, 13
Tale of Johnny Town-Mouse, The, 15
Tale of Peter Rabbit, The, 13

Tale of the Earl of Mar's
  Daughter, The, 63
Talk, 63
Talkative Tortoise, The, 46
Talking Cat, The, 43
Talking Pot, The, 48
Tam Lin, 77
Tamara and the Sea Witch, 43
Tamlane, 77
Tears of the Dragon, The, 43
Teeny-Tiny, 77
Tell-Tale Heart, The, 63
Tengu's Magic Nose Fan, 43
Terrible Leak, The, 43
Terrible Stranger, The, 63
Thankful, 83
Theseus, 64
Third Lamb, The, 71
This Is the Christmas, 71
Thor and Loki in the Giants' City, 64
Thor and the Giant King, 64
Thor . . . How the Thunderer Was
  Tricked, 64
Thorn Rose, 42
Thor's Unlucky Journey, 64
Thousandth Gift, The, 64
Three Bears, The, 14
Three Billy Goats Gruff, The, 14
Three Feathers, 54
Three Gifts, The, 34
Three Goats, The, 14
Three Gold Pieces, 43
Three Golden Hairs, The, 44
Three Golden Hairs of the King of the
  Cave Giants, The, 44
Three Golden Oranges, 44
Three Little Animals, 14
Three Little Pigs, The, 14
Three Little Pigs and the Ogre, The, 44
Three Men of Power—Evening,
  Midnight, and Sunrise, The, 64
Three Oranges, The, 44
Three Sillies, The, 44
Three Sneezes, The, 44

Three Wishes, The, 14
Tico and the Golden Wings, 15
Tiger Story, Anansi Story, 27
Tiger, the Brahman, and the
  Jackal, The, 44
Tiki-Tiki-Tembo, 45
Tikki Tikki Tembo, 45
Tilly Witch, 77
Timid Timothy, 15
Tinder Box, The, 45
Ting-a-ling's Visit to Turilira, 45
Tinker and the Ghost, The, 77
To Your Good Health!, 64
Toads and Diamonds, 45
Tom Thumb, 45
Tom Tit Tot, 40
Tomten, The, 15
Tony Di-Moany, 34
Too Much Noise, 11
Too Much Nose, 61
Torten's Christmas Secret, 72
Tortoise Talked, The, 46
Tot Botot and His Little Flute, 15
Toward the Sun, 53
Town Mouse and the Country
  Mouse, The, 15
Trapper's Tale of the First
  Birthday, The, 72
Traveling Musicians, The, 4
Travels of a Fox, The, 15
Trojan Horse, The, 65
Trojan War, The, 65
Truce of the Wolf, The, 41
Tsarina's Greatest Treasure, The, 64
Tug of War, A, 45
Tug of War, The, 45
Turnip, The, 15
Turtle Who Couldn't Stop
  Talking, The, 46
'Twas in the Moon of Wintertime, 72
Twelve Dancing Princesses, The, 46
Twelve Months, The, 80
Twist-Mouth Family, The, 15
Two Bottles, The, 36

Two of Everything, 46
Ugly Duckling, The, 46
Ungrateful Tiger, The, 44
Unlucky Shoes of Ali Abou, The, 46
Urashima Taro and the Princess of
  the Sea, 46
Usha, the Mouse-Maiden, 46
Valentine Box, The, 82
Valiant Little Tailor, The, 20
Valiant Tailor, The, 20
Vasilisa the Beautiful, 22
Velveteen Rabbit, The, 74
Visit from St. Nicholas, A, 70
Voice of the Great Bell, The, 63
Voyage of the Wee Red Cap, The, 72
Wait for William, 15
Wakaima and the Clay Man, 49
Wave, The, 20
Wee Christmas Cabin of
  Carn-na-ween, The, 72
Week of Sundays, A, 64
Well o' the World's End, The, 27
What Ailed the King, 64
What the Good Man Does Is
  Always Right, 29
What the Good Man Does Is Sure
  to Be Right, 29
What's in the Dark?, 15
When the Drum Sang, 46
When the Husband Stayed Home, 31
When the Root Children Wake Up, 16
Where Love Is, God Is, 72
Where Love Is, There God Is Also, 72
Where the Wild Things Are, 16
Which Was Witch?, 78
Whippety Stourie, 41
Whiskers of Ho Ho, The, 74
Whistle for Willie, 16
White Cat, The, 26
White Hen, The, 41
White Horse Girl and the Blue
  Wind Boy, The, 65
Whitebear Whittington, 24
Who Took the Farmer's Hat?, 16

Who Was Tricked?, 47
Why Cats Always Wash After Eating, 16
Why Cats and Dogs Don't Like Each Other, 47
Why Cats Wash After Meals, 16
Why Dogs Hate Cats, 47
Why the Bear Is Stumpy-tailed, 47
Why the Bear Sleeps All Winter, 47
Why the Carabao's Hoof Is Split, 47
Why the Cat and the Dog Cannot Live at Peace, 47
Why the Chimes Rang, 72
Why the Dog and the Cat Are Not Friends, 47
Why the Jackal Won't Speak to the Hedgehog, 16
Why the Robin Has a Red Breast, 31
Why the Sea Is Salt, 47
Why the Sea Moans, 65
Why the Sun and Moon Live in the Sky, 16
Why the Sun Was Late, 16
Why the Woodpecker Has a Long Nose, 48
Why Women Talk More than Men, 65
William Tell, 48
Winning of the Sword, The, 57
Wisdom of Solomon, The, 48
Wise King and the Little Bee, The, 48
Wise Man on the Mountain, The, 11
Wise Witness, The, 65

Wishing Table, the Gold Donkey, and the Cudgel-in-the-Sack, The, 34
Wishing Well, The, 72
Witches' Ride, The, 78
Witch's Magic Cloth, The, 48
Wobble the Witch Cat, 78
Woggle of Witches, A, 78
Wolf and the Seven Goats, The, 16
Wolf and the Seven Kids, The, 16
Wolf and the Seven Little Kids, The, 16
Wolf of Gubbio, The, 41
'Wolf! Wolf!', 4
Woman's Wit, 65
Wonderful Dragon of Timlin, The, 16
Wonderful Knapsack, The, 48
Wonderful Pear Tree, The, 48
Wonderful Pot, The, 48
Wonderful Stone, The, 18
Wonderful Tar-Baby, The, 48
Wonderful Wooden Peacock Flying Machine, The, 49
Wooden Horse, The, 65
Wooden Shoes of Little Wolff, The, 72
Woodman and the Goblins, The, 78
Worker in Sandalwood, The, 72
World in the Candy Egg, The, 74
Yanni, 49
Yellow Ribbon, The, 65
Yom Kipper, Day of Atonement, 79
You Never Can Tell, 65
Zezolla and the Date-Palm Tree, 22
Zini and the Witches, 78

Books Referred to
in the Foregoing Lists

The authority for this list is the catalog of the Carnegie Library of Pittsburgh.

Aardema, Verna. *Tales for the Third Ear from Equatorial Africa.* Dutton, 1969.
Abisch, Roz. *'Twas in the Moon of Wintertime: The First American Christmas Carol.* Prentice, 1969.
Adams, Adrienne. *A Woggle of Witches.* Scribner, 1971.
Adams, Kathleen, and Bacon, F. E., comps. *A Book of Giant Stories.* Dodd, 1926.
———. *A Book of Princess Stories.* Dodd, 1927.
Adshead, G. L. *Brownies—Hush!* Walck, 1938.
———. *Brownies—It's Christmas!* Walck, 1955.
———. *An Inheritance of Poetry.* Houghton, 1948.
Aesop. *The Aesop for Children.* Hale, 1919.
———. *Androcles and the Lion.* Watts, 1970.
———. *Fables from Aesop.* Retold by James Reeves. Walck, 1962.
———. *The Fables of Aesop.* Selected, told anew, and their history traced by Joseph Jacobs. Macmillan, 1964.
———. *The Town Mouse and the Country Mouse.* Illustrated by Paul Galdone. McGraw, 1971.
Afanasev, Alexei. *Salt: A Russian Tale.* Adapted by Harve Zemach. Follett, 1965.
Alden, R. M. *Why the Chimes Rang.* Illustrated by Rafaello Busoni. Bobbs, 1954.
———. *Why the Chimes Rang and Other Stories.* Bobbs, 1945.
Alegria, R. E. *The Three Wishes: A Collection of Puerto Rican Folktales.* Harcourt, 1969.
Alexander, Frances. *Pebbles from a Broken Jar.* Bobbs, 1963.
Alger, L. G. *All in the Morning Early.* Holt, 1963.
———. *By Loch and by Lin.* Holt, 1969.
———. *Gaelic Ghosts.* Holt, 1963.
———. *Ghosts Go Haunting.* Holt, 1965.

————. *Heather and Broom: Tales of the Scottish Highlands.* Holt, 1960.

————. *Thistle and Thyme.* Holt, 1962.

Ambrus, Victor. *The Little Cockerel.* Harcourt, 1968.

————. *The Sultan's Bath.* Harcourt, 1971.

Andersen, H. C. *Andersen's Fairy Tales.* Translated by Mrs. E. V. Lucas and Mrs. H. B. Paull. Grosset, 1945.

————. *The Emperor's New Clothes.* Harcourt, 1959.

————. *Fairy Tales.* World, 1946.

————. *The Fir Tree.* Illustrated by Nancy Ekholm Burkert. Harper, 1970.

————. *It's Perfectly True and Other Stories.* Harcourt, 1938.

————. *The Little Match Girl.* Illustrated by Blair Lent. Houghton, 1968.

————. *The Nightingale.* Illustrated by Harold Berson. Lippincott, 1962.

————. *The Nightingale.* Translated by Eva Le Gallienne, illustrated by Nancy Ekholm Burkert. Harper, 1965.

————. *The Nightingale and the Emperor.* Harvey, 1970.

————. *The Steadfast Tin Soldier.* Scribner, 1953.

————. *The Swineherd.* Harcourt, 1958.

————. *The Ugly Duckling.* Macmillan, 1967.

————. *What the Good Man Does Is Always Right.* Illustrated by Rick Schreiter. Dial, 1968.

Arabian Nights' Entertainments. *The Arabian Nights.* Edited by Padraic Colum. Macmillan, 1964.

————. *Arabian Nights.* Edited by Andrew Lang. McKay, 1946.

————. *The Arabian Nights: Tales of Wonder and Magnificence.* Edited by Padraic Colum. Macmillan, 1953.

————. *The Arabian Nights: Their Best-Known Tales.* Edited by K. D. Wiggin and N. A. Smith. Scribner, 1909.

————. *The Black Monkey and Other Unfamiliar Tales from The Arabian Nights,* by John Hampden. Deutsch, 1968.

Arbuthnot, M. H. *Time for Fairy Tales, Old and New.* Rev. ed. Scott, 1961.

————. *Time for Poetry.* 3rd ed. Scott, 1968.

Arkhurst, J. C. *The Adventures of Spider: West African Folk Tales.* Little, 1964.

Arnott, Kathleen. *African Myths and Legends.* Walck, 1962.

Artzybasheff, Boris. *The Seven Simeons: A Russian Tale.* Viking, 1961.

Aruego, José. *A Crocodile's Tale.* Scribner, 1972.

Asbjörnsen, P. C. *The Three Billy Goats Gruff.* Illustrated by Marcia Brown. Harcourt, 1957.

————. *The Three Billy Goats Gruff.* Illustrated by Paul Galdone. Seabury, 1973.

————. *The Three Billy Goats Gruff.* Illustrated by William Stobbs. McGraw, 1968.

Asbjörnsen, P.C., and Moe, J.E. *East of the Sun and West of the Moon and Other Tales.* Macmillan, 1963.

————. *Favorite Fairy Tales Told in Norway.* Retold by Virginia Haviland. Little, 1961.

────. *Norwegian Folk Tales*. Viking, 1961.
Association for Childhood Education International. *Told Under the Blue Umbrella*. Macmillan, 1962.
────. *Told Under the Christmas Tree*. Macmillan, 1962.
────. *Told Under the Green Umbrella*. Macmillan, 1935.
────. *Told Under the Magic Umbrella*. Macmillan, 1967.
Atlantic Monthly, The, 104 (Dec. 1909), 786.
Aulaire, I. M. d', and E. P. d'. *Abraham Lincoln*. Doubleday, 1957.
────. *D'Aulaires' Book of Greek Myths*. Doubleday, 1962.
────. *Don't Count Your Chicks*. Doubleday, 1943.
────. *George Washington*. Doubleday, 1936.
Aulnoy, M. C. d'. *The White Cat and Other Old French Fairy Tales*. Macmillan, 1967.
Averill, Esther. *Jenny's Birthday Book*. Harper, 1954.
Bailey, C. S. *Children of the Handcrafts*. Viking, 1935.
Bailey, C. S., and Lewis, C. M., eds. *Favorite Stories for the Children's Hour*. Platt, 1965.
Baker, Augusta. *The Golden Lynx and Other Tales*. Lippincott, 1960.
────. *The Talking Tree: Fairy Tales from 15 Lands*. Lippincott, 1955.
Baldwin, A. N. *Sunflowers for Tina*. Four Winds, 1970.
Baldwin, James. *Favorite Tales of Long Ago*. Dutton, 1955.
────. *The Story of Roland*. Scribner, 1930.
────. *The Story of Siegfried*. Scribner, 1931.
Balet, Jan. *The Gift: A Portuguese Christmas Tale*. Delacorte, 1967.
Barbeau, Marius. *The Golden Phoenix, and Other French-Canadian Fairy Tales*. Walck, 1958.
Barksdale, L. E. *The First Thanksgiving*. Knopf, 1942.
Barlow, Genevieve. *Latin American Tales from the Pampas to the Pyramids of Mexico*. Rand, 1966.
Belpré, Pura. *Dance of the Animals: A Puerto Rican Folk Tale*. Warne, 1972.
────. *Oté: A Puerto Rican Folk Tale*. Pantheon, 1969.
────. *The Tiger and the Rabbit and Other Tales*. Lippincott, 1965.
Bemelmans, Ludwig. *Madeline*. Viking, 1939.
Benét, S. V. *The Ballad of William Sycamore*. Little, 1972.
Benson, Sally. *Stories of the Gods and Heroes*. Dial, 1940.
Berson, Harold. *Why the Jackal Won't Speak to the Hedgehog*. Seabury, 1969.
Beskow, Elsa. *Pelle's New Suit*. Harper, 1929.
Bianco, M. W. *The Velveteen Rabbit*. Doubleday, 1958.
Bible—New Testament.
Bible—New Testament. *The Christ Child*, as told by Matthew and Luke. Illustrated by Maud and Miska Petersham. Doubleday, 1931.
Bible—Old Testament.
Bishop, C. H. *The Five Chinese Brothers*. Coward, 1938.
────. *Happy Christmas! Tales for Boys and Girls*. Ungar, 1956.

————. The Man Who Lost His Head. Viking, 1942.
Bleecker, M. N. Big Music or Twenty Merry Tales to Tell. Viking, 1946.
Boggs, R. S., and Davis, M. G. Three Golden Oranges and Other Spanish Folk Tales. McKay, 1936.
Bolliger, Max. The Golden Apple: A Story. Atheneum, 1970.
Borski, L. M. Good Sense and Good Fortune and Other Polish Folk Tales. McKay, 1970.
Borski, L. M., and Miller, K. B. The Jolly Tailor and Other Fairy Tales. McKay, 1957.
Botkin, B. A. A Treasury of American Folklore. Crown, 1944.
Bowie, W. R. The Bible Story for Boys and Girls: Old Testament. Abingdon, 1952.
Bowman, J. C. Pecos Bill: The Greatest Cowboy of All Time. Whitman, 1937.
————. Who Was Tricked? Whitman, 1966.
Bowman, J. C., and Bianco, M. W. Tales from a Finnish Tupa. Whitman, 1936.
Brandenberg, Aliki. The Eggs. Pantheon, 1969.
————. Three Gold Pieces. Pantheon, 1967.
Bright, Robert. Georgie to the Rescue. Doubleday, 1956.
————. Richard Brown and the Dragon. Doubleday, 1952.
Brock, E. L. The Runaway Sardine. Knopf, 1929.
Brockett, Eleanor. Burmese and Thai Fairy Tales. Follett, 1967.
————. Persian Fairy Tales. Follett, 1968.
Brooke, L. L. The Golden Goose Book. Warne, 1905.
Brooks, W. R. Jimmy Takes Vanishing Lessons. Knopf, 1965.
Broun, Heywood. The Fifty-First Dragon. Prentice, 1968.
Brown, Marcia. The Bun. Harcourt, 1972.
————. Dick Whittington and His Cat. Scribner, 1950.
————. The Neighbors. Scribner, 1967.
————. Stone Soup. Scribner, 1947.
Brown, M. W. The Golden Egg Book. Golden Press, 1972.
————. The Runaway Bunny. Harper, 1970.
————. Three Little Animals. Harper, 1956.
Browne, Frances. Granny's Wonderful Chair. Macmillan, 1963.
Browning, Robert. The Pied Piper of Hamelin. Warne, 1889.
Bruderhof Communities. Behold That Star: A Christmas Anthology. Plough, 1966.
Brustlein, Janice. Little Bear's Thanksgiving. Lothrop, 1967.
Bryant, S. C. How to Tell Stories to Children. Houghton, 1924. Reprint. Gale, 1971.
Buck, P. S. The Chinese Story Teller. Day, 1971.
————. Fairy Tales of the Orient. Simon, 1965.
Buff, Mary, and Conrad. The Apple and the Arrow. Houghton, 1951.
Bulfinch, Thomas. A Book of Myths. Illustrated by Helen Sewell. Macmillan, 1942.

Burningham, John. *Mr. Gumpy's Outing.* Cape, 1970.

Burton, V. L. *The Little House.* Houghton, 1942.

———. *Mike Mulligan and His Steam Shovel.* Houghton, 1939.

Calhoun, Mary. *The Goblin Under the Stairs.* Morrow, 1968.

———. *The Hungry Leprechaun.* Morrow, 1962.

———. *Wobble the Witch Cat.* Morrow, 1958.

Carey, M. C. *Fairy Tales of Long Ago.* Dutton, 1952.

Carlson, N. S. *The Talking Cat and Other Stories of French Canada.* Harper, 1952.

Carmer, C. L. *America Sings.* Knopf, 1950.

———. *A Cavalcade of Young Americans.* Lothrop, 1958.

———. *Hurricane's Children.* McKay, 1967.

Carpenter, Frances. *African Wonder Tales.* Doubleday, 1963.

———. *The Elephant's Bathtub: Wonder Tales from the Far East.* Doubleday, 1962.

———. *South American Wonder Tales.* Follett, 1969.

———. *Tales of a Chinese Grandmother.* Doubleday, 1937.

———. *Tales of a Korean Grandmother.* Tuttle, 1972.

———. *Wonder Tales of Dogs and Cats.* Doubleday, 1955.

———. *Wonder Tales of Horses and Heroes.* Doubleday, 1952.

Cathon, L. E. *Tot Botot and His Little Flute.* Macmillan, 1970.

Cathon, L. E., and Schmidt, Thusnelda. *Perhaps and Perchance: Tales of Nature.* Abingdon, 1962.

———. *Treasured Tales: Great Stories of Courage and Faith.* Abingdon, 1960.

Chaikin, Miriam. *Ittki Pittki.* Parents', 1971.

Chang, I. C. *Chinese Fairy Tales.* Schocken, 1968.

———. *Tales from Old China.* Random, 1969.

Chappell, Warren. *The Nutcracker.* Knopf, 1958.

Chase, Richard. *Grandfather Tales: American-English Folk Tales.* Houghton, 1948.

———. *The Jack Tales: Folk Tales from the Southern Appalachians.* Houghton, 1943.

Chaucer, Geoffrey. *The Franklin's Tale.* Retold by Ian Serraillier. Warne, 1972.

Child Study Association of America. *Castles and Dragons.* Crowell, 1958.

———. *Holiday Storybook.* Crowell, 1952.

Chrisman, A. B. *Shen of the Sea: Chinese Stories for Children.* Dutton, 1968.

Chroman, Eleanor. *It Could Be Worse.* Childrens, 1972.

Clark, Margery. *The Poppy Seed Cakes.* Doubleday, 1924.

Cole, William. *The Poet's Tales: A New Book of Story Poems.* World, 1971.

Colum, Padraic. *The Children of Odin: The Book of Northern Myths.* Macmillan, 1948.

———. *The Golden Fleece and the Heroes Who Lived Before Achilles.* Macmillan, 1962.

Colwell, Eileen. *A Second Storyteller's Choice: A Selection of Stories, with Notes on How to Tell Them.* Walck, 1965.
———. *A Storyteller's Choice: A Selection of Stories, with Notes on How to Tell Them.* Walck, 1964.
———. *Tell Me a Story: A Collection for Under Five.* Penguin, 1962.
———. *Tell Me Another Story.* Penguin, 1964.
Cook, R. J. *One Hundred and One Famous Poems.* Reilly, 1958.
Coolidge, O. E. *Greek Myths.* Houghton, 1949.
———. *Legends of the North.* Houghton, 1951.
Cooney, Barbara. *Chanticleer and the Fox,* by Geoffrey Chaucer. Crowell, 1958.
———. *The Little Juggler.* Adapted from an old French legend. Hastings, 1961.
Cothran, Jean. *With a Wig, with a Wag, and Other American Folk Tales.* McKay, 1954.
Courlander, Harold, and Herzog, George. *The Cow-Tail Switch and Other West African Stories.* Holt, 1947.
Courlander, Harold, and Leslau, Wolf. *The Fire on the Mountain and Other Ethiopian Stories.* Holt, 1950.
Credle, Ellis. *Down down the Mountain.* Nelson, 1934.
———. *Tall Tales from the High Hills and Other Stories.* Nelson, 1957.
Dalgliesh, Alice. *The Columbus Story.* Scribner, 1955.
———. *The Enchanted Book.* Scribner, 1947.
———. *Ride on the Wind.* Adapted from *The Spirit of St. Louis,* by Charles A. Lindbergh. Scribner, 1956.
———. *The Thanksgiving Story.* Scribner, 1954.
Danaher, Kevin. *Folktales of the Irish Countryside.* White, 1970.
Daniels, Guy. *The Falcon Under the Hat: Russian Merry Tales and Fairy Tales.* Funk, 1969.
Daugherty, J. H. *Andy and the Lion.* Viking, 1938.
Davis, M. G. *A Baker's Dozen: Thirteen Stories to Tell and to Read Aloud.* Harcourt, 1930.
Dayrell, Elphinstone. *Why the Sun and Moon Live in the Sky.* Houghton, 1968.
De La Mare, W. J. *Animal Stories.* Scribner, 1940.
———. *Stories from the Bible.* Knopf, 1961.
———. *Tales Told Again.* Knopf, 1959.
De Paola, Tomie. *The Wonderful Dragon of Timlin.* Bobbs, 1966.
De Regniers, B. S. *David and Goliath.* Viking, 1965.
———. *May I Bring a Friend?* Atheneum, 1964.
Deutsch, Babette, and Yarmolinsky, Avrahm. *More Tales of Faraway Folk.* Harper, 1963.
———. *Tales of Faraway Folk.* Harper, 1952.
Devlin, Wende, and Harry. *Cranberry Thanksgiving.* Parents', 1971.
Dillon, Eilís. *The Wise Man on the Mountain.* Atheneum, 1969.

Diverting Adventures of Tom Thumb, The. Illustrated by Barry Wilkinson. Harcourt, 1967.

Dobbs, Rose. *No Room*. McKay, 1944.

———. *Once Upon a Time*. Random, 1958.

Dodge, M. M. *Hans Brinker or the Silver Skates*. Scribner, 1915.

Dolbier, Maurice. *Torten's Christmas Secret*. Little, 1951.

Domanska, Janina. *Look, There Is a Turtle Flying*. Macmillan, 1968.

———. *The Turnip*. Macmillan, 1969.

Du Bois, W. P. *Elisabeth the Cow Ghost*. Viking, 1964.

———. *Otto and the Magic Potatoes*. Viking, 1970.

Durham, Mae. *Tit for Tat and Other Latvian Folk Tales*. Harcourt, 1967.

Duvoisin, R. A. *One Thousand Christmas Beards*. Knopf, 1955.

———. *The Three Sneezes and Other Swiss Tales*. Knopf, 1941.

Eaton, A. T. *The Animals' Christmas*. Viking, 1944.

Elkin, Benjamin. *Why the Sun Was Late*. Parents', 1966.

———. *The Wisest Man in the World: A Legend of Ancient Israel*. Parents', 1968.

Emrich, Duncan. *An Almanac of American Folklore: The Hodgepodge Book*. Four Winds, 1972.

Ets, M. H. *In the Forest*. Viking, 1944.

———. *Play with Me*. Viking, 1955.

Eulenspiegel, Tyll. *Tyll Ulenspiegel's Merry Pranks*. Vanguard, 1938.

Evans, Katherine. *The Boy Who Cried Wolf*. Whitman, 1960.

———. *A Bundle of Sticks*. Whitman, 1962.

———. *The Maid and Her Pail of Milk*. Whitman, 1959.

Farjeon, Eleanor. *The Little Bookroom*. Walck, 1956.

———. *Mighty Men*. Appleton, 1947.

———. *The Old Nurse's Stocking-Basket*. Walck, 1965.

Fatio, Louise. *The Happy Lion*. McGraw, 1954.

Felt, Sue. *Rosa-Too-Little*. Doubleday, 1950.

Felton, H. W. *Legends of Paul Bunyan*. Knopf, 1947.

Fenner, P. R. *Adventure: Rare and Magical*. Knopf, 1945.

———. *Demons and Dervishes*. Knopf, 1946.

———. *Feasts and Frolics: Special Stories for Special Days*. Knopf, 1949.

———. *Fools and Funny Fellows: More "Time to Laugh" Tales*. Knopf, 1947.

———. *Ghosts, Ghosts, Ghosts*. Watts, 1952.

———. *Giants & Witches and a Dragon or Two*. Knopf, 1943.

———. *Princesses & Peasant Boys*. Knopf, 1944.

———. *Time to Laugh: Funny Tales from Here and There*. Knopf, 1942.

Ferris, Helen. *Favorite Poems Old and New*. Doubleday, 1957.

Field, R. L. *American Folk and Fairy Tales*. Scribner, 1929.

Fillmore, Parker. *The Shepherd's Nosegay: Stories from Finland and Czechoslovakia*. Harcourt, 1958.

Finger, C. J. Tales from Silver Lands. Doubleday, 1924.

Finlay, Winifred. Folk Tales from the North. Watts, 1969.

Fish, H. D. The Boy's Book of Verse. Lippincott, 1951.

Fisher, A. B. Stories California Indians Told. Parnassus, 1957.

Fisher, A. L. My Mother and I. Crowell, 1967.

Fitzgerald, B. S. World Tales for Creative Dramatics and Storytelling. Prentice, 1962.

Flack, Marjorie. Angus and the Ducks. Doubleday, 1939.

———. Ask Mr. Bear. Macmillan, 1958.

———. Wait for William. Houghton, 1935.

Flack, Marjorie, and Wiese, Kurt. The Story About Ping. Viking, 1933.

Flora, James. Little Hatchy Hen. Harcourt, 1969.

Forbes, Esther. Mama's Bank Account. Harcourt, 1949.

Foster, Genevieve. Abraham Lincoln. Scribner, 1950.

———. George Washington. Scribner, 1949.

Foulds, E. V. The Elephant and the Bad Baby. Coward, 1970.

Freehof, L. B. Stories of King Solomon. Jewish Publication Society, 1955.

Freeman, Don. Corduroy. Viking, 1968.

———. Dandelion. Viking, 1964.

———. Space Witch. Viking, 1959.

———. Tilly Witch. Viking, 1969.

Friedrich, Priscilla, and Otto. The Easter Bunny That Overslept. Lothrop, 1957.

Frost, F. M. Legends of the United Nations. McGraw, 1943.

Gág, Wanda. The Funny Thing. Coward, 1920.

———. Gone Is Gone. Coward, 1935.

———. Millions of Cats. Coward, 1938.

Gagliardo, Ruth. Let's Read Aloud. Lippincott, 1962.

Galdone, Paul. The Monkey and the Crocodile: A Jataka Tale from India. Seabury, 1969.

Gamoran, M. G. Hillel's Happy Holidays. Union of American Hebrew Congregations, 1955.

Garrett, Helen. Angelo, the Naughty One. Viking, 1944.

Gates, Doris. Lord of the Sky: Zeus. Viking, 1972.

———. The Warrior Goddess: Athena. Viking, 1972.

Geisel, T. S. The 500 Hats of Bartholomew Cubbins. Vanguard, 1938.

———. The Lorax. Random, 1971.

Gobhai, Mehlli. The Legend of the Orange Princess. Holiday, 1971.

———. Usha, the Mouse-Maiden. Hawthorn, 1969.

Godden, Rumer. The Mousewife. Viking, 1951.

———. The Old Woman Who Lived in a Vinegar Bottle. Viking, 1972.

Graham, A. P. Christopher Columbus, Discoverer. Abingdon, 1950.

Graham, G. B. The Beggar in the Blanket & Other Vietnamese Tales. Dial, 1970.

Grahame, Kenneth. The Reluctant Dragon. Holiday, 1953.

Gramatky, Hardie. *Little Toot.* Putnam, 1939.

Green, Lila. *Folktales and Fairy Tales of Africa.* Silver, 1967.

Green, Nancy. *The Bigger Giant: An Irish Legend.* Follett, 1963.

Green, R. L. *Modern Fairy Stories.* Dutton, 1956.

————. *Tales of Make-Believe.* Dutton, 1960.

Grimm, J. L., and W. K. *The Bremen Town Musicians.* Illustrated by Paul Galdone. McGraw, 1968.

————. *The Elves and the Shoemaker.* Illustrated by Katrin Brandt. Follett, 1968.

————. *Fairy Tales.* Translated by Mrs. E. V. Lucas et al. Grosset, 1945.

————. *Fairy Tales.* Illustrated by Jean O'Neill. World, 1947.

————. *Favorite Fairy Tales Told in Germany.* Retold by Virginia Haviland. Little, 1959.

————. *The Fisherman and His Wife.* Illustrated by Margot Zemach. Norton, 1966.

————. *The Four Musicians.* Doubleday, 1968.

————. *The Golden Goose.* Illustrated by William Stobbs. McGraw, 1967.

————. *Grimms' Fairy Tales.* Illustrated by Fritz Kredel. Grosset, 1945.

————. *Grimms' Fairy Tales.* Illustrated by Arnold Roth. Macmillan, 1963.

————. *Grimms' Fairy Tales.* Illustrated by Ulrik Schramm. Walck, 1962.

————. *Hansel and Gretel.* Knopf, 1944.

————. *The House in the Wood.* Warne, 1910.

————. *Household Stories.* McGraw, 1966.

————. *Jorinda and Joringel.* Illustrated by Adrienne Adams. Scribner, 1968.

————. *King Thrushbeard.* Illustrated by Felix Hoffmann. Harcourt, 1969.

————. *King Thrushbeard.* Retold and illustrated by Kurt Werth. Viking, 1968.

————. *More Tales from Grimm.* Translated by Wanda Gág. Coward, 1947.

————. *Nibble Nibble Mousekin.* Illustrated by Joan Walsh Anglund. Harcourt, 1962.

————. *Rumpelstiltskin.* Illustrated by William Stobbs. Walck, 1970.

————. *The Shoemaker and the Elves.* Illustrated by Adrienne Adams. Scribner, 1960.

————. *The Sleeping Beauty.* Illustrated by Felix Hoffmann. Harcourt, 1959.

————. *Snow White and the Seven Dwarfs.* Coward, 1938.

————. *Snow-White and the Seven Dwarfs.* Illustrated by Nancy Ekholm Burkert. Farrar, 1972.

————. *Tales from Grimm.* Translated by Wanda Gág. Coward, 1936.

————. *Three Gay Tales.* Coward, 1943.

————. *Tom Thumb.* Illustrated by Felix Hoffmann. Atheneum, 1973.

————. *The Traveling Musicians.* Harcourt, 1955.

————. *The Twelve Dancing Princesses.* Illustrated by Uri Shulevitz. Scribner, 1966.

————. *The Valiant Little Tailor.* Illustrated by Anne Marie Jauss. Harvey, 1967.

————. *The Wolf and the Seven Little Kids.* Harcourt, 1959.

Gruenberg, S. M. *Favorite Stories Old and New.* Rev. ed. Doubleday, 1955.
Guirma, Frederic. *Princess of the Full Moon.* Macmillan, 1970.
Hader, Berta, and Elmer. *The Mighty Hunter.* Macmillan, 1943.
————. *The Story of Pancho and the Bull with the Crooked Tail.*
    Macmillan, 1942.
Hale, L. P. *The Peterkin Papers.* Doubleday, 1955.
Haley, G. E. *A Story, a Story: An African Tale.* Atheneum, 1970.
Hamada, Hirosuke. *The Tears of the Dragon.* Parents', 1967.
Hampden, John. *The Gypsy Fiddle and Other Tales Told by Gypsies.*
    World, 1969.
————. *The House of Cats & Other Stories.* Farrar, 1967.
Handforth, Thomas. *Mei Li.* Doubleday, 1938.
Hardendorff, J. B. *The Frog's Saddle Horse and Other Tales.* Lippincott, 1968.
————. *Just One More.* Lippincott, 1969.
————. *Slip! Slop! Gobble!* Lippincott, 1970.
————. *Tricky Peik and Other Picture Tales.* Lippincott, 1967.
Harper, Wilhelmina. *Easter Chimes: Stories for Easter and the Spring Season.*
    Rev. ed. Dutton, 1965.
————. *Ghosts and Goblins: Stories for Hallowe'en and Other Times.*
    Rev. ed. Dutton, 1965.
————. *The Gunniwolf.* Dutton, 1967.
————. *The Harvest Feast: Stories of Thanksgiving Yesterday and Today.*
    Rev. ed. Dutton, 1965.
————. *Merry Christmas to You! Stories for Christmas.* Rev. ed. Dutton, 1965.
Harris, J. C. *The Favorite Uncle Remus.* Houghton, 1948.
Harris, Rosemary. *The Child in the Bamboo Grove.* Phillips, 1971.
Hatch, M. C. *More Danish Tales.* Harcourt, 1949.
————. *13 Danish Tales.* Harcourt, 1947.
Haviland, Virginia. *The Fairy Tale Treasury.* Coward, 1972.
————. *Favorite Fairy Tales Told in Czechoslovakia.* Little, 1966.
————. *Favorite Fairy Tales Told in India.* Little, 1973.
————. *Favorite Fairy Tales Told in Ireland.* Little, 1961.
————. *Favorite Fairy Tales Told in Norway.* Little, 1961.
————. *Favorite Fairy Tales Told in Poland.* Little, 1963.
————. *Favorite Fairy Tales Told in Russia.* Little, 1961.
————. *Favorite Fairy Tales Told in Spain.* Little, 1963.
————. *Favorite Fairy Tales Told in Sweden.* Little, 1966.
Hawthorne, Nathaniel. *The Golden Touch.* McGraw, 1959.
————. *A Wonder Book and Tanglewood Tales.* Dodd, 1934.
Hazeltine, A. I. *Children's Stories to Read or Tell.* Abingdon, 1949.
————. *Hero Tales from Many Lands.* Abingdon, 1961.
Hazeltine, A. I., and Smith, E. S. *The Easter Book of Legends and Stories.*
    Lothrop, 1947.

Hearn, Lafcadio. *The Boy Who Drew Cats and Other Tales.* Macmillan, 1963.
———. *Japanese Fairy Tales.* Peter Pauper, 1958.
Hewett, Anita. *The Little White Hen.* McGraw, 1963.
Heyward, Du Bose. *The Country Bunny and the Little Gold Shoes.* Houghton, 1939.
Hieatt, Constance. *Sir Gawain and the Green Knight.* Crowell, 1967.
Hitchcock, Alfred. *Alfred Hitchcock's Haunted Houseful.* Random, 1961.
Hitopadésa. *Once a Mouse.* Illustrated by Marcia Brown. Scribner, 1961.
Hoban, Russell. *Bedtime for Frances.* Harper, 1960.
Hodges, Margaret. *The Fire Bringer: A Paiute Indian Legend.* Little, 1972.
———. *The Gorgon's Head: A Myth from the Isles of Greece.* Little, 1972.
———. *The Other World: Myths of the Celts.* Farrar, 1973.
———. *Persephone and the Springtime.* Little, 1973.
———. *Tell It Again: Great Tales from Around the World.* Dial, 1963.
———. *The Wave.* Houghton, 1964.
Hoff, Sydney. *Herschel the Hero.* Putnam, 1969.
———. *Lengthy.* Putnam, 1964.
Hogrogian, Nonny. *One Fine Day.* Macmillan, 1971.
Hogstrom, D. D. *One Silver Second: A Fable for All Ages.* Rand, 1972.
Hoke, H. L. *Witches, Witches, Witches.* Watts, 1966.
Holding, James. *The King's Contest and Other North African Tales.* Abelard, 1964.
Holl, Adelaide. *The Remarkable Egg.* Lothrop, 1968.
Holland, Janice. *You Never Can Tell.* Scribner, 1963.
Hollowell, Lillian. *A Book of Children's Literature.* 3rd ed. Holt, 1966.
Horn Book Magazine, The, 20, no. 6 (Nov.–Dec. 1944), 501–09.
Hosford, D. G. *By His Own Might: The Battles of Beowulf.* Holt, 1947.
———. *Thunder of the Gods.* Holt, 1952.
Hosier, John. *The Sorcerer's Apprentice and Other Stories.* Walck, 1961.
House That Jack Built, The. Illustrated by Randolph Caldecott. Warne, 1878.
———. Illustrated by Paul Galdone. McGraw, 1961.
———. Illustrated by Rodney Peppé. Delacorte, 1970.
———. Illustrated by Joe Rogers. Lothrop, 1967.
Huber, M. B. *Story and Verse for Children.* 3rd ed. Macmillan, 1965.
Huffard, G. T. *My Poetry Book: An Anthology of Modern Verse for Boys and Girls.* Rev. ed. Holt, 1956.
Hughes, R. A. *The Spider's Palace and Other Stories.* Random, 1960.
Hurd, E. T. *The So-So Cat.* Harper, 1965.
Hurlbut, J. L. *Hurlbut's Story of the Bible for Young and Old.* Zondervan, 1967.
Hürlimann, Bettina. *William Tell and His Son.* Harcourt, 1967.
Hurlong, L. F. *Adventures of Jabotí on the Amazon.* Abelard, 1968.
Hutchins, Pat. *Good Night, Owl!* Macmillan, 1972.
———. *Rosie's Walk.* Macmillan, 1968.

———. *The Surprise Party*. Macmillan, 1969.
Hutchinson, V. S. *Candlelight Stories*. Putnam, 1928.
———. *Chimney Corner Fairy Tales*. Putnam, 1926.
———. *Chimney Corner Stories: Tales for Little Children*. Putnam, 1905.
———. *Fireside Stories*. Putnam, 1927.
Ipcar, Dahlov. *The Cat at Night*. Doubleday, 1969.
Irving, Washington. *The Alhambra: Palace of Mystery and Splendor*.
    Macmillan, 1953.
———. *The Bold Dragoon and Other Ghostly Tales*. Knopf, 1930.
———. *Rip Van Winkle and the Legend of Sleepy Hollow*. Macmillan, 1963.
Ishii, Momoko. *Issun Boshi, the Inchling: An Old Tale of Japan*. Walker, 1967.
Jablow, Alta, and Withers, Carl. *The Man in the Moon: Sky Tales from
    Many Lands*. Holt, 1969.
Jack and the Beanstalk. Illustrated by William Stobbs. Delacorte, 1969.
Jacobs, Francine. *The Legs of the Moon*. Coward, 1971.
Jacobs, Joseph. *The Buried Moon*. Bradbury, 1969.
———. *Celtic Folk and Fairy Tales*. Putnam, 1905.
———. *English Folk and Fairy Tales*. Putnam, 1904.
———. *Favorite Fairy Tales Told in England*. Retold by Virginia Haviland.
    Little, 1959.
———. *Henny-Penny*. Illustrated by Paul Galdone. Seabury, 1968.
———. *Henny-Penny*. Illustrated by William Stobbs. Follett, 1968.
———. *Hudden and Dudden and Donald O'Neary*. Coward, 1968.
———. *More English Folk and Fairy Tales*. Putnam, 1904.
———. *The Pied Piper and Other Fairy Tales*. Macmillan, 1968.
———. *The Three Wishes*. Illustrated by Paul Galdone. McGraw, 1961.
Jagendorf, M. A. *Noodlehead Stories from Around the World*. Vanguard, 1957.
———. *The Priceless Cats and Other Italian Folk Stories*. Vanguard, 1956.
———. *Upstate, Downstate: Folk Stories of the Middle Atlantic States*.
    Vanguard, 1949.
Jagendorf, M. A., and Tillhagen, C. H. *The Gypsies' Fiddle and Other
    Gypsy Tales*. Vanguard, 1956.
Jameson, Cynthia. *One for the Price of Two*. Parents', 1972.
Jātakas. *Jataka Tales: Animal Stories*. Retold by E. C. Babbitt. Appleton, 1912.
———. *More Jataka Tales: Animal Stories*. Retold by E. C. Babbitt.
    Appleton, 1922.
Jauss, A. M. *Legends of Saints and Beasts*. American Book, 1954.
Jewett, E. M. *Which Was Witch? Tales of Ghosts and Magic from Korea*.
    Viking, 1953.
Jewett, Sophie. *God's Troubadour: The Story of Saint Francis of Assisi*.
    Crowell, 1957.
Johnson, Clifton. *The Oak-Tree Fairy Book: Favorite Fairy Tales*. Dover, 1968.
Johnson, Edna; Sickels, E. R.; and Sayers, F. C., eds. *Anthology of
    Children's Literature*. 4th rev. ed. Houghton, 1970.

Johnson, S. P. *The Harper Book of Princes.* Harper, 1964.
———. *The Princesses: Sixteen Stories About Princesses.* Harper, 1962.
Johnston, Johanna. *Edie Changes Her Mind.* Putnam, 1964.
Jones, E. O. *Maminka's Children.* Macmillan, 1968.
Jones, Gwyn. *Scandinavian Legends and Folk-Tales.* Walck, 1956.
Kahl, Virginia. *Away Went Wolfgang!* Scribner, 1954.
Karrick, V. V. *Still More Russian Picture Tales.* Dover, 1970.
Keats, E. J. *John Henry: An American Legend.* Pantheon, 1965.
———. *The Snowy Day.* Viking, 1962.
———. *Whistle for Willie.* Viking, 1964.
Kelsey, A. G. *Once the Hodja.* McKay, 1943.
Kent, Jack. *The Fat Cat: A Danish Folktale.* Parents', 1971.
Kimishima, Hisako. *Ma Lien and the Magic Brush.* Parents', 1968.
———. *The Princess of the Rice Fields: An Indonesian Folk Tale.* Walker, 1970.
Kingsley, Charles. *The Heroes: Greek Fairy Tales.* Macmillan, 1954.
Kipling, Rudyard. *The Elephant's Child.* Illustrated by Leonard Weisgard. Walker, 1970.
———. *The Jungle Book.* Doubleday, 1932.
———. *Just So Stories.* Doubleday, 1946.
———. *Just So Stories.* Illustrated by Etienne Delessert. Doubleday, 1972.
———. *Just So Stories.* Illustrated by Nicholas. Doubleday, 1946.
Koshland, Ellen. *The Magic Lollipop.* Knopf, 1971.
Kramer, Caroline. *Read-Aloud Nursery Tales.* Random, 1957.
La Fontaine, Jean de. *The Lion and the Rat.* Watts. 1964.
Lang, Andrew. *Blue Fairy Book.* McKay, 1948.
———. *Blue Fairy Book.* Random, 1959.
———. *Crimson Fairy Book.* McKay, 1947.
———. *Green Fairy Book.* McGraw, 1966.
———. *Green Fairy Book.* McKay, 1948.
———. *Grey Fairy Book.* Peter Smith, n.d.
———. *Lilac Fairy Book.* Peter Smith, n.d.
———. *Red Fairy Book.* McKay, 1950.
———. *The Twelve Dancing Princesses.* Illustrated by Adrienne Adams. Holt, 1966.
———. *Violet Fairy Book.* McGraw, 1967.
———. *Violet Fairy Book.* McKay, 1951.
———. *Yellow Fairy Book.* McKay, 1951.
Lawson, Robert. *I Discover Columbus.* Little, 1941.
Lazarus, K. F. *The Billy Goat in the Chili Patch.* Steck, 1970.
Leach, Maria. *The Rainbow Book of American Folk Tales and Legends.* World, 1958.
Leach, Maria. *The Soup Stone.* Funk, 1954.
Leaf, Munro. *The Story of Ferdinand.* Viking, 1936.
Lefèvre, Félicité. *The Cock, the Mouse and the Little Red Hen.* Macrae, 1947.

Lester, Julius. *The Knee-High Man and Other Tales.* Dial, 1972.
Le Sueur, Meridel. *Little Brother of the Wilderness: The Story of Johnny Appleseed.* Knopf, 1947.
Lindgren, Astrid. *The Tomten.* Coward, 1961.
Lines, K. M. *Nursery Stories.* Watts, 1960.
———. *Tales of Magic and Enchantment.* Transatlantic, 1967.
Lionni, Leo. *Frederick.* Pantheon, 1967.
———. *Inch by Inch.* Obolensky, 1960.
———. *Tico and the Golden Wings.* Pantheon, 1964.
Lipkind, William. *The Magic Feather Duster.* Harcourt, 1958.
Littlefield, William. *The Whiskers of Ho Ho.* Lothrop, n.d.
Lobel, Arnold. *Prince Bertram the Bad.* Harper, 1963.
Longfellow, H. W. *Poems of Henry Wadsworth Longfellow.* Selected by Edmund Fuller. Crowell, 1967.
Lovelace, M. H. *The Valentine Box.* Crowell, 1966.
Lowe, P. T. *The Little Horse of Seven Colors and Other Portuguese Folk Tales.* World, 1970.
Luckhardt, M. M. *Thanksgiving: Feast and Festival.* Abingdon, 1966.
Lum, Peter. *Italian Fairy Tales.* Follett, 1963.
Lyons, Grant. *Tales the People Tell in Mexico.* Messner, 1972.
Maas, Selve. *The Moon Painters and Other Estonian Folk Tales.* Viking, 1971.
McCloskey, Robert. *Blueberries for Sal.* Viking, 1948.
———. *Homer Price.* Viking, 1943.
———. *Make Way for Ducklings.* Viking, 1941.
McCormick, D. J. *Paul Bunyan Swings His Axe.* Caxton, 1936.
McDermott, Gerald. *The Magic Tree: A Tale from the Congo.* Holt, 1973.
McDowell, R. E., and Lavitt, Edward. *Third World Voices for Children.* Third Press, 1971.
McGinley, Phyllis. *How Mrs. Santa Claus Saved Christmas.* Lippincott, 1963.
———. *The Plain Princess.* Lippincott, 1945.
McGovern, Ann. *Too Much Noise.* Houghton, 1967.
MacManus, Seumas. *The Bold Heroes of Hungry Hill and Other Irish Folk Tales.* Farrar, 1951.
McPhail, D. M. *The Bear's Toothache.* Little, 1972.
Malcolmson, A. B. *Song of Robin Hood.* Houghton, 1947.
———. *Yankee Doodle's Cousins.* Houghton, 1941.
Malory, Sir Thomas. *The Boy's King Arthur.* Edited by Sidney Lanier. Scribner, 1917.
Manifold, L.F. *The Christmas Window.* Houghton, 1971.
Manning-Sanders, Ruth. *A Book of Charms and Changelings.* Dutton, 1971.
———. *A Book of Dragons.* Dutton, 1965.
———. *A Book of Giants.* Dutton, 1963.
———. *A Book of Magical Beasts.* Nelson, 1970.
———. *A Book of Wizards.* Dutton, 1967.

———. Stories from the English and Scottish Ballads. Dutton, 1968.
Matsutani, Miyoko. The Fisherman Under the Sea. Parents', 1969.
———. The Witch's Magic Cloth. Parents', 1969.
Mayne, William. William Mayne's Book of Heroes: Stories and Poems. Dutton, 1968.
Mehdevi, Alexander. Bungling Pedro & Other Majorcan Tales. Knopf, 1970.
Memling, Carl. What's in the Dark? Parents', 1971.
Milhous, Katherine. Appolonia's Valentine. Scribner, 1954.
———. The Egg Tree. Scribner, 1950.
Miller, Alan. I Know an Old Lady. Rand, 1961.
Minarik, E. H. Little Bear. Harper, 1957.
Molin, Charles. Ghosts, Spooks, & Spectres. White, 1967.
Monsell, H. A. Paddy's Christmas. Knopf, 1942.
Moore, C. C. The Night Before Christmas. Lippincott, 1954.
Morrow, Betty. A Great Miracle: The Story of Hanukkah. Harvey, 1968.
Mosel, Arlene. The Funny Little Woman. Dutton, 1972.
———. Tikki Tikki Tembo. Holt, 1968.
Mother Goose, Nursery Rhyme Book. Edited by Andrew Lang. Rev. ed. Warne, 1897.
Müller-Guggenbühl, Fritz. Swiss-Alpine Folk-Tales. Walck, 1958.
Ness, Evaline. The Girl and the Goatherd or This and That and Thus and So. Dutton, 1970.
———. Long, Broad, & Quickeye. Scribner, 1969.
Neufeld, Rose. Beware the Man Without a Beard and Other Greek Tales. Knopf, 1969.
Nixon, K. I. Animal Legends. Warne, 1966.
Nodset, Joan. Who Took the Farmer's Hat? Harper, 1963.
Noyes, Alfred. The Highwayman. Prentice, 1969.
O'Faolain, Eileen. Irish Sagas and Folktales. Walck, 1954.
Olcott, F. J. Good Stories for Great Holidays. Houghton, 1914.
———. Story-Telling Poems. Books for Libraries, 1970.
Old Woman and Her Pig, The. Illustrated by Paul Galdone. McGraw, 1960.
Olfers, Sibylle von. When the Root Children Wake Up. Lippincott, n.d.
Olsen, I. S. Smoke. Coward, 1972.
Pannell, Lucile, and Cavanah, Frances. Holiday Round Up. Rev. ed. Macrae, 1968.
Panter, Carol. Beany and His New Recorder. Four Winds, 1972.
Pauli, H. E. Silent Night, the Story of a Song. Knopf, 1943.
Pearce, Philippa. Beauty and the Beast. Crowell, 1972.
Peck, Leigh. Pecos Bill and Lightning. Houghton, 1940.
Perrault, Charles. Cinderella. Illustrated by Marcia Brown. Scribner, 1954.
———. Favorite Fairy Tales Told in France. Retold by Virginia Haviland. Little, 1959.
———. Puss in Boots. Illustrated by Marcia Brown. Harcourt, 1959.

————. *Puss in Boots.* Illustrated by Hans Fischer. Scribner, 1952.
Petersham, Maud, and Miska. *The Circus Baby.* Macmillan, 1950.
————. *David.* Macmillan, 1967.
————. *Joseph and His Brothers.* Macmillan, 1958.
————. *Moses.* Macmillan, 1958.
Phumla, Mbane. *Nomi and the Magic Fish: A Story from Africa.* Doubleday, 1972.
Picard, B. L. *French Legends, Tales, and Fairy Stories.* Walck, 1955.
————. *German Hero-Sagas and Folk-Tales.* Walck, 1958.
————. *The Mermaid and the Simpleton.* Criterion, 1970.
————. *Tales of Ancient Persia.* Walck, 1972.
Pilkington, F. M. *Shamrock and Spear: Tales and Legends from Ireland.* Holt, 1968.
Piper, Watty. *The Little Engine That Could.* Platt, 1954.
Poe, E. A. *The Pit and the Pendulum and Five Other Tales.* Watts, 1967.
————. *Tales and Poems.* Macmillan, 1967.
Politi, Leo. *Juanita.* Scribner, 1948.
————. *Saint Francis and the Animals.* Scribner, 1959.
Potter, Beatrix. *The Tailor of Gloucester.* Warne, 1903.
————. *The Tale of Johnny Town-Mouse.* Warne, 1918.
————. *The Tale of Peter Rabbit.* Warne, 1904.
Power, Effie. *Bag O' Tales.* Singing Tree, 1968.
Preston, E. M. *One Dark Night.* Viking, 1969.
Price, Christine. *The Rich Man and the Singer: Folktales from Ethiopia.* Dutton, 1971.
————. *Sixty at a Blow: A Tall Tale from Turkey.* Dutton, 1968.
Price, M. E. *Myths and Enchantment Tales.* Rand, 1960.
Pridham, Radost. *A Gift from the Heart.* World, 1967.
Prokofiev, S. S. *Peter and the Wolf.* Illustrated by Warren Chappell. Knopf, 1940.
Protter, Eric. *Gypsy Tales.* Lion, 1967.
Provensen, Alice, and Martin. *The Provensen Book of Fairy Tales.* Random, 1971.
Pugh, Ellen. *Tales from the Welsh Hills.* Dodd, 1968.
Pyle, Howard. *King Stork.* Little, 1973.
————. *The Merry Adventures of Robin Hood.* Scribner, 1946.
————. *Pepper & Salt; or, Seasoning for Young Folk.* Harper, 1913.
————. *Some Merry Adventures of Robin Hood.* Scribner, 1954.
————. *The Story of King Arthur and His Knights.* Scribner, 1903.
————. *Twilight Land.* Peter Smith, n.d.
————. *The Wonder Clock.* Harper, 1915.
Quigley, Lillian. *The Blind Men and the Elephant.* Scribner, 1959.
Quinn, Zdenka, and J. P. *The Water Sprite of the Golden Town: Folk Tales of Bohemia.* Macrae, 1971.

Rackham, Arthur. *The Arthur Rackham Fairy Book.* Lippincott, 1950.
Ranke, Kurt. *Folktales of Germany.* University of Chicago, 1966.
Ransome, Arthur. *The Fool of the World and the Flying Ship.* Farrar, 1968.
————. *Old Peter's Russian Tales.* Dover, 1969.
————. *Old Peter's Russian Tales.* Nelson, 1938.
Raymond, Louise. *Famous Myths of the Golden Age.* Random, 1947.
Reesink, Maryke. *Peter and the Twelve-Headed Dragon.* Harcourt, 1970.
Reeves, James. *English Fables and Fairy Stories.* Walck, 1954.
————. *The Trojan Horse.* Watts, 1969.
Reid, D. M. *Tales of Nanabozho.* Walck, 1963.
Rey, H. A. *Curious George Takes a Job.* Houghton, 1947.
Reyher, Rebecca. *My Mother Is the Most Beautiful Woman in the World.*
    Lothrop, 1945.
Ritchie, Alice. *The Treasure of Li-Po.* Harcourt, 1949.
Robbins, Ruth. *Baboushka and the Three Kings.* Parnassus, 1960.
Robertson, D. L. *Fairy Tales from Viet Nam.* Dodd, 1968.
Roche, A. K. *The Clever Turtle.* Prentice, 1969.
Rockwell, A. F. *The Stolen Necklace: A Picture Story from India.* World, 1968.
————. *When the Drum Sang: An African Folktale.* Parents', 1970.
Ross, E. S. *The Blue Rose: A Collection of Stories for Girls.* Harcourt, 1966.
————. *The Buried Treasure and Other Picture Tales.* Lippincott, 1958.
————. *The Lost Half-Hour: A Collection of Stories.* Harcourt, 1963.
Rounds, Glen. *Ol' Paul, the Mighty Logger.* Holiday, 1949.
Rudolph, Marguerita. *I Am Your Misfortune.* Seabury, 1968.
Rugoff, M. A. *A Harvest of World Folk Tales.* Viking, 1949.
Ruskin, John. *The King of the Golden River.* World, 1946.
Sandburg, Carl. *Rootabaga Stories.* Harcourt, 1923.
Savory, Phyllis. *Lion Outwitted by Hare and Other African Tales.*
    Whitman, 1971.
Sawyer, Ruth. *Journey Cake, Ho!* Viking, 1953.
————. *Joy to the World.* Little, 1966.
————. *The Long Christmas.* Viking, 1941.
————. *This Is the Christmas: A Serbian Folk Tale.* Horn Book, 1945.
————. *This Way to Christmas.* Harper, 1967.
————. *The Way of the Storyteller.* Viking, 1962.
Saxe, J. G. *The Blind Men and the Elephant.* McGraw, 1963.
Schatz, Letta. *The Extraordinary Tug-of-War.* Follett, 1968.
Schauffler, R. H., ed. and comp. *The Days We Celebrate: Celebrations for
    Festivals.* Vol. 2. Dodd, 1940.
Schiller, Barbara. *The Kitchen Knight.* Holt, 1965.
Schmitt, Gladys. *The Heroic Deeds of Beowulf.* Random, 1962.
Schoolcraft, H. R. *The Ring in the Prairie: A Shawnee Legend.* Dial, 1970.
Scott, A. H. *Sam.* McGraw, 1967.
Sechrist, E. H. *Heigh-Ho for Halloween!* Macrae, 1948.

————. Once in the First Times: Folk Tales from the Philippines. Macrae, 1969.
————. Thirteen Ghostly Yarns. Macrae, 1963.
Sechrist, E. H., and Woolsey, Janette. It's Time for Christmas. Macrae, 1959.
————. It's Time for Story Hour. Macrae, 1964.
————. It's Time for Thanksgiving. Macrae, 1957.
Seignobosc, Françoise. Noël for Jeanne-Marie. Scribner, 1953.
Sellew, C. F. Adventures with the Giants. Little, 1950.
————. Adventures with the Gods. Little, 1945.
Sendak, Maurice. Where the Wild Things Are. Harper, 1963.
Seredy, Kate. The Good Master. Viking, 1935.
Serraillier, Ian. The Challenge of the Green Knight. Walck, 1967.
Shannon, Monica. Dobry. Viking, 1934.
Shapiro, Irwin. Heroes in American Folklore. Messner, 1962.
————. Yankee Thunder: The Legendary Life of Davy Crockett. Messner, 1944.
Shedlock, M. L. The Art of the Story-Teller. Dover, 1951.
Sheehan, Ethna. Folk and Fairy Tales from Around the World. Dodd, 1970.
————. A Treasury of Catholic Children's Stories. Lippincott, 1963.
Sherlock, P.M. Anansi, the Spider Man: Jamaican Folk Tales. Crowell, 1954.
————. West Indian Folk-Tales. Walck, 1966.
Sherman, H. A., and Kent, C. F. The Children's Bible. Scribner, 1922.
Shippen, K. B. A Bridle for Pegasus. Viking, 1951.
————. The Great Heritage. Viking, 1947.
Shivkumar, K. The King's Choice. Parents', 1971.
Shulevitz, Uri. The Magician. Adapted from the Yiddish of I. L. Peretz.
    Macmillan, 1973.
————. Rain, Rain Rivers. Farrar, 1969.
Simon, Sidney. The Armadillo Who Had No Shell. Norton, 1966.
Singer, I. B. When Shlemiel Went to Warsaw & Other Stories. Farrar, 1968.
————. Zlateh the Goat and Other Stories. Harper, 1966.
Sivulich, S. S. I'm Going on a Bear Hunt. Dutton, 1973.
Sleator, William. The Angry Moon. Little, 1970.
Sleigh, Barbara. North of Nowhere: Stories and Legends from Many Lands.
    Collins, 1966.
Slobodkina, Esphyr. Caps for Sale. Young Scott, 1947.
Smith, E. S. Mystery Tales for Boys and Girls. Lothrop, 1946.
Smith, E. S., and Hazeltine, A. I. The Christmas Book of Legends & Stories.
    Lothrop, 1944.
————. Just for Fun: Humorous Stories and Poems. Lothrop, 1948.
Smith, H. R. Laughing Matter. Scribner, 1949.
Spellman, J. W. The Beautiful Blue Jay and Other Tales of India. Little, 1967.
Spicer, D. G. The Kneeling Tree and Other Folk Tales from the Middle East.
    Coward, 1971.
————. Long Ago in Serbia. Westminster, 1968.
Steel, F. A. English Fairy Tales. Macmillan, 1962.

————. *The Tiger, the Brahman, and the Jackal.* Holt, 1963.

Stein, R. C. *Steel Driving Man: The Legend of John Henry.* Childrens, 1969.

Stevens, James. *Paul Bunyan.* Knopf, 1948.

Stockton, F. R. *Ting-a-ling Tales.* Scribner, 1955.

Story of the Three Little Pigs, The. Illustrated by William Stobbs. McGraw, 1965.

Stoutenburg, Adrien. *American Tall Tales.* Viking, 1966.

Suddeth, R. E., and Morenus, C. G. *Tales of the Western World.* Steck, 1954.

Sutcliff, Rosemary. *Beowulf.* Bodley Head, 1961.

Tall Book of Christmas, The. Harper, 1954.

Tashjian, V. A. *Once There Was and Was Not: Armenian Tales.* Little, 1966.

————. *Three Apples Fell from Heaven.* Little, 1971.

Taylor, Mark. *The Fisherman and the Goblet.* Golden Gate, 1971.

Taylor, Sydney. *All-of-a-Kind Family.* Follett, 1951.

————. *More All-of-a-Kind Family.* Follett, 1954.

Tazewell, Charles. *The Littlest Angel.* Childrens, 1946.

Temple, Shirley. *Shirley Temple's Storytime Favorites.* Random, 1962.

Thompson, Stith. *One Hundred Favorite Folk Tales.* Indiana University, 1968.

Thurber, James. *The Great Quillow.* Harcourt, 1944.

————. *Many Moons.* Harcourt, 1943.

Todd, M. F. *The Juggler of Notre Dame: An Old French Tale.* McGraw, 1954.

Tolstoi, A. N. *The Great Big Enormous Turnip.* Watts, 1968.

Tom Tit Tot: An English Folk Tale. Illustrated by Evaline Ness. Scribner, 1965.

Toor, Frances. *The Golden Carnation and Other Stories Told in Italy.* Lothrop, 1960.

Tooze, Ruth. *The Wonderful Wooden Peacock Flying Machine and Other Tales of Ceylon.* Day, 1969.

Travers, P. L. *Mary Poppins.* Harcourt, 1934.

Tresselt, A. R. *The Mitten: An Old Ukrainian Folktale.* Lothrop, 1964.

————. *The World in the Candy Egg.* Lothrop, 1967.

Tresselt, A. R., and Cleaver, Nancy. *The Legend of the Willow Plate.* Parents', 1968.

Troughton, Joanna. *Sir Gawain and the Loathly Damsel.* Dutton, 1972.

Tudor, Tasha. *Tasha Tudor's Favorite Stories.* Lippincott, 1965.

Turska, Krystyna. *Pegasus.* Watts, 1970.

————. *Tamara and the Sea Witch.* Parents', 1971.

Uchida, Yoshiko. *The Dancing Kettle and Other Japanese Folk Tales.* Harcourt, 1949.

————. *The Magic Listening Cap: More Folk Tales from Japan.* Harcourt, 1955.

————. *The Sea of Gold and Other Stories from Japan.* Scribner, 1965.

Undset, Sigrid. *True and Untrue and Other Norse Tales.* Knopf, 1945.

Untermeyer, Louis. *Big and Little Creatures.* Golden Press, 1962.

————. *The Firebringer and Other Great Stories: Fifty-Five Legends That Live Forever.* Lippincott, 1968.

————. *The Golden Treasury of Poetry.* Golden Press, 1959.

———. Magic Circle: Stories & People in Poetry. Harcourt, 1952.
———. The World's Great Stories: Fifty-Five Legends That Live Forever. Lippincott, 1964.
Van Thal, Herbert. Famous Tales of the Fantastic. Hill, 1965.
Vance, Marguerite. A Star for Hansi. Dutton, 1957.
Vasilisa the Beautiful. Translated by Thomas P. Whitney. Macmillan, 1970.
Von Hippel, Ursula. The Craziest Hallowe'en. Coward, 1957.
Wahl, Jan. The Animals' Peace Day. Crown, 1970.
Walden, Daniel. The Nutcracker. Adapted from the ballet by Lev Ivanov and Peter Ilich Tchaikovsky. Lippincott, 1959.
Walker, B. K. The Dancing Palm Tree and Other Nigerian Folktales. Parents', 1968.
———. How the Hare Told the Truth About His Horse. Parents', 1972.
———. The Ifrit and the Magic Gifts. Follett, 1972.
———. Once There Was and Twice There Wasn't. Follett, 1967.
Ward, Winifred. Stories to Dramatize. Anchorage, 1952.
Watson, J. W. The Mysterious Gold and Purple Box. Garrard, 1972.
Watson, K. W. Tales for Telling. Wilson, 1950.
Watts, Mabel. A Cow in the House. Follett, 1956.
Weisgard, Leonard. The Plymouth Thanksgiving. Doubleday, 1967.
Wernecke, H. H. Christmas Stories from Many Lands. Westminster, 1961.
Werth, Kurt. Lazy Jack. Viking, 1970.
———. Molly and the Giant. Parents', 1973.
———. The Valiant Tailor. Viking, 1965.
Westwood, Jennifer. Medieval Tales. Coward, 1968.
Wheeler, Opal. Sing for Christmas: A Round of Christmas Carols and Stories of the Carols. Dutton, 1943.
Wiesner, William. Happy-Go-Lucky. Seabury, 1970.
———. Joco and the Fishbone: An Arabian Nights Tale. Viking, 1966.
Wiggin, K. D., and Smith, N. A. The Fairy Ring. Rev. ed. Doubleday, 1967.
Wilde, Oscar. The Complete Fairy Tales of Oscar Wilde. Watts, 1960.
———. The Happy Prince. Illustrated by Gilbert Riswold. Prentice, 1965.
———. The Happy Prince and Other Stories. Dutton, 1968.
———. The Selfish Giant and Other Stories. Kenedy, 1954.
Wildsmith, Brian. The Owl and the Woodpecker. Watts, 1971.
Wilkins, M. E. The Pumpkin Giant. Retold by Ellin Greene. Lothrop, 1970.
Williams, Gweneria. Timid Timothy. Young Scott, 1944.
Williams-Ellis, Amabel. Fairy Tales from the British Isles. Warne, 1964.
Wilson, B. K. Scottish Folk-Tales and Legends. Walck, 1954.
Winter, Jeanette. The Christmas Visitors: A Norwegian Folktale. Pantheon, 1968.
Withers, Carl. I Saw a Rocket Walk a Mile. Holt, 1965.
Wolkstein, Diane. 8,000 Stones: A Chinese Folktale. Doubleday, 1972.
Wondriska, William. Mr. Brown and Mr. Gray. Holt, 1968.
Woolley, Catherine. The Outside Cat. Morrow, 1957.

Worm, Piet. *More Stories from the Old Testament*. Sheed, 1958.
———. *Stories from the Old Testament*. Sheed, 1956.
Wright, Dare. *The Lonely Doll*. Doubleday, 1957.
Wyndham, Robert. *Tales the People Tell in China*. Messner, 1971.
Yezback, S. A. *Pumpkinseeds*. Bobbs, 1969.
Yoda, Junichi. *The Rolling Rice Ball*. Parents', 1969.
Yolen, J. H. *The Emperor and the Kite*. World, 1967.
Young, B. C. *How the Manx Cat Lost Its Tail and Other Manx Folk Stories*. McKay, 1959.
Young, Miriam. *Miss Suzy's Easter Surprise*. Parents', 1972.
Zajdler, Zoë. *Polish Fairy Tales*. Follett, 1968.
Zemach, Harve. *Nail Soup: A Swedish Folk Tale*. Follett, 1964.
———. *Too Much Nose: An Italian Tale*. Holt, 1967.
Zemach, Margot. *The Three Sillies*. Holt, 1963.
Zinkin, Taya. *The Faithful Parrot and Other Indian Folk Stories*. Watts, 1968.
Zion, Gene. *Harry the Dirty Dog*. Harper, 1956.
Zolotow, Charlotte. *Mr. Rabbit and the Lovely Present*. Harper, 1962.